The Love of Clitophon and Leucippe

The Love of Clitophon and Leucippe

Achilles Tatius

MINT EDITIONS

The Love of Clitophon and Leucippe was first published in 1597.

This edition published by Mint Editions 2021.

ISBN 9781513277547 | E-ISBN 9781513277950

Published by Mint Editions®

 MINT
EDITIONS

minteditionbooks.com

Publishing Director: Jennifer Newens
Design & Production: Rachel Lopez Metzger
Project Manager: Micaela Clark
Translated by: Rowland Smith
Typesetting: Westchester Publishing Services

Contents

Book I

S idon is situated upon the coast of the Assyrian sea; it is the mother city of the Phœnicians, and its inhabitants were the founders of Thebes. It has a harbour of capacious extent, which gradually admits within it the waters of the sea; it is double, because, to the right, a passage has been dug into an inner basin, which likewise admits the sea; in this manner the first harbour becomes the entrance to a second, which affords a secure haven to vessels during summer, while in winter they can ride at anchor safely in the former. Upon arriving here after encountering a severe storm, I made thank-offerings on account of my preservation, to the goddess of the Phœnicians, called by the Sidonians, Astarte. As I was wandering about the city, surveying the votive offerings in the temples, I saw a painting containing a view both of sea and land. Europa formed the subject, and the scene was laid partly on the Phœnician sea, partly on the coast of Sidon. In a meadow was seen a band of maidens; a bull was swimming in the sea, directing his course towards Crete, and having a fair damsel seated upon his back. The meadow was diversified with flowers intermixed with trees and shrubs; the trees were near to one another, and their branches and leaves united so closely overhead, as to form a cover for the flowers below. The artist had shewn great skill in managing the shade; for the sun-rays were seen dispersedly breaking through the overarching roof of leaves, and lighting up the meadow, which, situated as I have said, beneath a leafy screen, was surrounded on all sides by a hedge. Under the trees, beds of flowers were laid out, in which bloomed the narcissus, the rose, and the myrtle. Bubbling up from the ground, a stream flowed through the midst of this enamelled meadow, watering the flowers and shrubs; and a gardener was represented with his pickaxe opening a channel for its course. The maidens above mentioned were placed by the painter, in a part of the meadow bordering upon the sea. Their countenances wore a mingled expression of joy and fear; they had chaplets upon their heads, their hair fell dishevelled about their shoulders; their legs were entirely bare—for a cincture raised their garments above the knee—and their feet were unsandalled; their cheeks were pale and contracted through alarm; their eyes were directed towards the sea; their lips were slightly opened as if about to give vent to their terror in cries; their hands were stretched out towards the bull; they were represented upon the verge of the sea, the water just coming over their feet; they appeared eager to hasten after the bull, but at the same time fearful of encountering the waves. The colour of the sea was twofold: towards the land it had a ruddy hue; farther out it was dark blue; foam also, and rocks and waves were represented; the rocks projecting from the shore, and whitened with foam, caused by the crests of the waves breaking upon their rugged surface.

In the midst of the sea, the bull was represented swimming, the waves rising in mountains from the motion of his legs. The maiden was seated upon his back, not astride, but sideways; she grasped his horn with her left hand, as a charioteer would hold the reins; and the bull inclined his head in that direction, as if guided by her hand.

She was dressed in a white tunic as far as her middle, the rest of her body was clothed in a purple robe; the whole dress, however, was so transparent as to disclose the beauties of her person. You could discern the deep-seated navel, the well proportioned stomach, the narrow waist, gradually widening until it reached the chest, the gently budding breasts.—These, as well as the tunic, were confined by a cincture, and from its transparency, the tunic became, so to speak, a mirror to reflect her person. Both her hands were extended, one towards the horn, the other towards the tail; and with either of them she held an extremity of the veil which was expanded above her shoulders, and which appeared in every part inflated by the artist's "painted wind."

Thus seated upon the bull, the maiden resembled a vessel in full sail, her veil serving for the canvass. Dolphins leaped, Loves sported round the bull; you might have sworn that they moved "instinct with life." Cupid, in person, was drawing on the bull; Cupid, in guise of a little child, was spreading his wings, bearing his quiver, holding his torch, and turning towards Jove, was archly laughing as if in mockery of him, who, on his account had become a bull.

I admired every part of this painting, but my attention was more especially rivetted upon Cupid leading forward the bull; and I exclaimed, "How wonderfully does a mere child lord it over heaven and earth and sea!"

Upon this, a young man, who happened to be standing near, said, "I can speak from experience of the power of Love, having suffered so severely from his caprices."—"Pray," said I, "what are the ills which you have suffered? To speak the truth, your countenance betokens you to be not unacquainted with the mysteries of this deity."—"You are stirring up a whole swarm of words," replied he, "mystery will sound like a fable."—"In the name of Jupiter and Love himself, my good fellow," rejoined I, "do not hesitate to gratify my curiosity, however fabulous may seem your story."

After this, taking him by the hand, I led him to a neighbouring grove, thickly planted with plane trees, through which flowed a stream of water, cold and transparent as that which proceeds from newly melted snow. Having placed him upon a low seat, I sat down beside him, and said, "Now is the time for hearing your tale; this spot is in every way agreeable and exactly suited for a love story." Upon this, he began as follows:—

I am a native of Phœnicia, was born at Tyre, and am named Clitopho; my father's name is Hippias; Sostratus is the name of his brother by the father's side—for the two had different mothers—the latter having a Byzantian, the former a Tyrian lady for his mother. Sostratus always resided at Byzantium, having inherited large property in that city from his mother; my father lived at Tyre. I never saw my mother, she having died during my infancy: after her decease, my father married a second wife, by whom he had a daughter named Calligone, whom he designed to unite to me in marriage. The will of the Fates, however, more powerful than that of men, had in store for me a different wife. Now, the Deity is often wont to reveal the future to mortals, in dreams by night; not in order that they may ward off suffering (for it is impossible to defeat destiny), but that they may bear more lightly their load of evils. Calamity, when it comes suddenly and in a "whole battalion," paralyses, and, as it were, overwhelms the soul by its unexpectedness, whereas when anticipated and dwelt upon by the mind, the edge of grief becomes blunted. It was when I had reached the age of nineteen, and when my father was preparing to have my marriage celebrated, the following year, that the drama of my fate began. During my sleep, in thought I had coalesced with, and *grown* into, the person of a maiden, as far as the middle, and that from thence upward we formed two bodies. A tall and terrible-looking woman, savage in aspect, with blood-shot eyes, inflamed cheeks, and snaky hair, stood over us. In her right hand she held a scimitar, in her left, a torch. Angrily raising her falchion, she let it fall exactly upon the loins where was the juncture of our bodies, and severed the maiden from me. Leaping up in terror, I mentioned the dream to no one, but foreboded evil in my own mind. Meanwhile, a messenger arrived from Byzantium, bringing a letter from my father's brother; it contained the following words:—

"Sostratus to his brother Hippias, sends greeting,

"My daughter Leucippe, and my wife Panthea, are on their way to you, for war has broken out between the Thracians and Byzantians; till it is concluded, keep under your protection those dearest objects of my affection. Farewell."

No sooner had my father read the letter than, rising from his seat, he hurried down to the harbour; and not long after returned, followed by a number of male and female slaves, whom Sostratus had sent with his wife and daughter. Among them was a tall lady, richly dressed: while looking at her, I remarked at her left hand, a maiden, the beauty of whose countenance at once dazzled my eyes—she resembled the Europa, whom, in the picture I had seen sitting upon the bull. Her sparkling eyes had a pleasing expression, her hair was golden-hued, short and curling, her eyebrows were jet black, her cheeks were fair, save that in the middle they had a tinge bordering upon purple, like that with which the Lydian women stain the ivory; her mouth was like the rose when it begins to bud. No sooner did I see her than my fate was sealed—for beauty inflicts a wound sharper than any arrow, finding a passage to the soul through the eyes, for it is the eye which makes a way for the wounds of love. I was overwhelmed by conflicting feelings; admiration, astonishment, agitation, shame, assurance: I admired her figure, I was astonished at her beauty; my heart palpitated, I gazed upon her with assurance, yet I was ashamed at the idea of being remarked. I endeavoured to withdraw my eyes from the maiden; they however were unwilling to obey, and, following the fascination of her countenance, in the end completely gained the day.

Upon the arrival of the visitors, my father assigned a part of the house for their use, and then ordered the supper to be prepared. At the appointed time we reclined by twos on couches, for such was my father's order. He and I were in the centre, the two elder ladies occupied the right-hand couch, the maidens were to the left. Upon hearing the proposed arrangement I was very near embracing my father, for thus placing the maiden within my view. As to what I ate, on my faith I cannot tell you, for I was like a man eating in a dream; all I know is, that leaning upon my elbow, and bending forwards, my whole attention was given to stealing furtive glances at her—this was the sum total of my supper. When the meal was ended, a slave came in with the lyre; he first ran over the strings with his fingers, then sounded a few chords in an under tone, and afterwards taking the plectrum, began to play, accompanying the sounds with his voice. The subject of his strain was

Apollo in his irritation pursuing the flying Daphne, and upon the point of seizing her, how she was transformed into a laurel, and how the god crowns himself with its leaves. The song had the effect of adding fuel to my flame, for amatory strains act as a powerful incentive to desire: and however inclined a person may be to chastity, example serves as a stimulant to imitation, more especially when the example is supplied by one in superior station; for the feeling of shame which was a check upon doing wrong becomes changed into assurance by the rank of the offender.

Accordingly, I thus reasoned with myself—"See, Apollo falls in love, he is not ashamed of his weakness, he pursues the fair one! and art thou a laggard and the slave of shame and ill-timed continence? Art thou, forsooth, superior to a god?" In the evening the ladies retired to rest first, and afterwards we ourselves. The others had confined the pleasures of the table to their stomachs. I, for my part, carried away the banquet in my eyes; I had taken my fill of the maiden's sweet looks, and, from the effect of merely gazing upon her, I rose from table intoxicated with love. Upon entering my accustomed chamber, sleep was out of the question. It is the law of nature that diseases and bodily wounds always become exasperated at night; when we are taking our rest their strength increases, and the pain becomes more acute, for the circumstance of the body being in repose affords leisure for the malady to do its work. By the same rule, the wounds of the soul are much more painful while the body is lying motionless; in the day, both the eyes and ears are occupied by a multiplicity of objects; thus, the soul has not leisure to feel pain, and so the violence of the disease is for a time mitigated; but let the body be fettered by inactivity, and then the soul retains all its susceptibility, and becomes tempest-tossed by trouble; the feelings which were asleep then awaken. The mourner feels his grief, the anxious his solicitude, he who is in peril his terrors, the lover his inward flame.

Towards morning Love took compassion upon me, and granted me some short repose; but not even then would the maiden be absent from my mind; Leucippe was in all my dreams, I conversed with her, I played with her, I supped with her, I touched her fair body; in short, I obtained more favours then than in the day-time, for I kissed her, and the kiss was really given. Accordingly, when the slave awoke me, I cursed him for coming so unseasonably, and for dissipating so sweet a dream; getting up, however, I went out of my part of the house, and walked in front of the apartment where the maiden was; with my head hanging down over a book, I pretended to be reading, but whenever I came opposite her door I cast sidelong glances, and after taking a few turns, and drinking in fresh draughts of love I returned desperately smitten; three whole days did I continue burning with this inward fire.

I had a cousin named Clinias, who had lost both his parents; he was two years older than myself, and an adept in matters of love. He had a male favourite, for whom his affection was so strong, that when he had one day purchased a horse, and the other admired it, he immediately presented him with the animal. I was always joking him for having so much leisure as to fall in love, and for being a slave to tender passions; he used to laugh and reply with a shake of the head, "Depend upon it the day of slavery is in store for you." Well, proceeding to his house, I saluted him, and sitting down, said, "Clinias, I am paying the penalty of my former gibes; I am at last myself the slave of love!" Upon hearing this, he clapped his hands and laughed outright; then rising and kissing my face, which bore traces of a lover's wakefulness, "There is no doubt of your being in love," said he, "for your eyes declare it."

While he was yet speaking, Charicles, his favourite, comes in hurriedly and in great perturbation, exclaiming, "My fate is sealed, Clinias!" With a tremulous voice, and sighing as deeply as though his own life hung upon that of the youth, Clinias replied, "Speak out, your silence will be my death; say what grief assails you—with what adversary have you to contend?" Charicles rejoined,—"My father is negotiating a marriage for me, a marriage moreover with an ill-favoured woman; a double evil therefore: even were she comely, a female would be repulsive to my taste, and she becomes doubly so, if ugly. My father, however, looks only to money, and is therefore anxious for the match, so that I, such is my ill fate, am made the victim of this woman's money; I am sold to be her husband." Clinias turned pale upon hearing this announcement, and strongly urged the youth to decline the match, bitterly inveighing against the race of womankind. "Your father, forsooth, would have you marry! pray what crime have you committed, that you should be given over to such bondage? Do you not remember the words of Jove?

'Son of Iapetus, o'er-subtle, go,
And glory in thy artful theft below;
Now of the fire you boast by stealth retriev'd,
And triumph in almighty Jove deceiv'd;

But thou too late shalt find the triumph vain,
And read thy folly in succeeding pain;
Posterity the sad effect shall know,
When in pursuit of joy they grasp their woe.'

Woman is a 'bitter sweet;' in her nature she is akin to the Sirens, for they too, slay their victims with a dulcet voice; the very "pomp and circumstance" of marriage shews the magnitude of the evil; there is the din of pipes, the knocking at the doors, the bearing about of torches. With all this noise and tumult, who will not exclaim, 'Unhappy is the man who has to wed!'—to me, he seems like a man ordered off to war. Were you unacquainted with classic lore, you might plead ignorance of women's doings, whereas you are so well read, as to be capable of teaching others. How many subjects for the stage have been furnished by womankind! Call to mind the necklace of Eriphyle, the banquet of Philomela, the calumny of Sthenobœa, the incest of Aerope, the murderous deed of Procne. Does Agamemnon sigh for the beauty of Chryseis?—he brings pestilence upon the Grecian host; does Achilles covet the charms of Briseis?—he prepares misery for himself; if Candaules has a fair wife, that wife becomes the murderess of her husband! The nuptial torches of Helen kindled the fire which consumed Troy! How many suitors were done to death through the chastity of Penelope? Phædra, through love, became the destroyer of Hippolytus; Clytemnestra, through hate, the murderess of Agamemnon! O! all-audacious race of women! they deal death whether they love or hate! The noble Agamemnon must needs die, he whose beauty is described to have been cast in a heavenly mould,

'Jove o'er his eyes celestial glories spread,
And dawning conquest play'd around his head.

and yet this very head was cut off by—a woman! All that I have been saying relates only to the handsome among the sex; in this case, then, there is a lessening of the evil, for beauty is a palliative, and under such circumstances a man may be said to be fortunate in the midst of his calamity; but if, as you say, the woman boasts no charms, why then the evil becomes two-fold. Who would submit in such a case, especially who that is young and handsome like yourself? In the name of the gods, Charicles, do not stoop to such a yoke; do not mar the flower of your beauty before the time; for remember, in addition to the other ills of marriage, there is this evil, it saps the vigour: do not, Charicles, I pray, expose yourself to this; give not the beauteous rose to be plucked by the ill-favoured rustic's hand."

"Leave this matter," replied Charicles, "to the care of the gods and of myself; the marriage will not take place for some days yet; much may be done in a single night, and we will deliberate at our leisure. Meanwhile, I will go and take a ride, for since the day you gave me that fine horse, I have never made use of your kind present." With these words he left the house, little imagining that this his first ride was to be his last. After he was gone, I related every particular to Clinias, describing how my passion began; the arrival, the supper, the beauty of the maiden. Feeling, at last, how absurdly I was beginning to talk, I exclaimed, "Clinias, I can no longer endure this misery. Love has assailed me with such violence as to drive sleep from my eyes; I see no object but Leucippe; no one can suffer like myself, for the source of my trouble dwells with me under the same roof."

"What folly it is," replied Clinias, "for you who are so fortunate in love to talk after this fashion! You have no need to go to another person's doors; you do not require a go-between; fortune gives the loved object into your hands, brings her into your very house, and there sets her down. Other lovers are well content with catching a glimpse of the maiden for whom they sigh, and to gratify their eyes is with them no small good fortune; they consider themselves most favoured, indeed, if they can now and then exchange a word with their mistress. But what is your case? You continually see her, you continually hear her voice, you sup with her, you drink with her; and yet, fortunate that you are, you are complaining! You are guilty of base ingratitude towards love, and without the slightest cause. Do you not know that seeing the object whom you love gives far deeper pleasure than enjoying her? And why so? Because the eyes, when encountering each other, receive bodily impressions, as in a looking-glass, and the reflection of beauty glancing into the soul, begets union even in separation, and affords a pleasure not much inferior to corporeal intercourse, which, after all, is hollow and unsatisfying. I augur, moreover, that you will soon obtain the object of your wishes, for to be always in the society of the loved one, exerts a most persuasive power; the eye is a wondrous vehicle of love, and constant intercourse is most influential in begetting kindly feelings. Habit and the company of each other will tame savage beasts.

How much more will they act upon a woman's heart. Parity of age also has great weight with a maiden, and the animal passion which is felt in the flower of youth, added to the consciousness of being loved, very frequently call forth a return of tender feeling. Every maiden wishes to be thought beautiful, and exults in being loved; and approves the testimony borne by the lover to her beauty; because, if no one love her, she believes herself devoid of any personal charms. This one piece of advice I give you, make her feel certain that she is beloved, and she will soon follow your example in returning your affection."

"And how," asked I, "is this sage oracle of yours to be accomplished? Put me in the right way; you are more experienced than myself; you have been longer initiated in the mysteries of love. What am I to do? What am I to say? How am I to obtain her for whom I sigh? For my part I am ignorant how to set about the work."

"There is small need," replied Clinias, "to learn these matters from the mouths of others. Love is a self-taught master of his craft. No one teaches new-born babes where to find their food; they have already learnt by intuition, and know that a table has been spread for them by nature in their mothers' breasts. In like manner, the youth who for the first time is pregnant with love, needs no teaching to bring it to the birth; only let your pains have come on, and your hour have arrived, and though it be for the first time, you will not miscarry, but will be safely brought to bed, midwifed by the god himself. I will, however, give you a few common-place hints relating to matters which require general observance. Say nothing to the maiden directly bearing upon love; prosecute the wished-for consummation quietly. Youths and maidens are alike sensible of shame, and however much they may long for sexual enjoyment, they do not like to hear it talked of; they consider the disgrace of the matter to be altogether in the words. Matrons take pleasure even in the words. A maiden will show no objection to acts of dalliance upon her lover's part, but will express her willingness by signs and gestures; yet if you come directly to the point, and put the question to her, your very voice will alarm her ears; she will be suffused with blushes; she will turn away from your proposals; she will think an insult has been done her; and however willing to comply with your desires, she will be restrained by shame; for the pleasurable sensations excited by your words will make her consider herself to be submitting to the act. But when by other means you have brought her to a compliant mood, so that you can approach her with some degree of freedom, be as wise and guarded as though you were celebrating the mysteries; gently approach and kiss her: a kiss given by a lover to a willing mistress is a silent way of asking for her favours; and the same given to the fair one who is coy, is a supplication to relent. Even when maidens are themselves ready to comply, they often like some appearance of force to be employed, for the plea of seeming necessity will remove the shame of voluntary compliance upon their part. Do not be discouraged if she repulses your advances, but mark the manner of her repulse: all these matters require tact. If she persists in being uncompliant, use no force; for she is not yet in the right humour; but if she show signs of yielding, act still with proper caution, lest after all you should lose your labour."

"You have given me store of good advice," said I, "and may everything turn out successfully; nevertheless I sadly fear that success will prove the beginning of even greater calamity, by making me more desperately in love. What am I to do if my malady increase? I cannot marry, for I am already engaged to another maiden; my father, too, is very urgent with me to conclude the match, and he asks nothing but what is fair and reasonable. He does not barter me away like Charicles for gold; he does not wish me to marry either a foreigner or an ugly girl; he gives me his own daughter, a maiden of rare beauty, had I not seen Leucippe; but now I am blind to all other charms excepting hers, in short, I have eyes for her alone. I am placed midway between two contending parties; Love on one side, my father on the other; the latter wields his paternal authority, the former shakes his burning torch; how am I to decide the cause? Stern necessity and natural affection are opposed. Father, I wish to give a verdict for you, but I have an adversary too strong for me; he tortures and overawes the judge, he stands beside me with his shafts; his arguments are flame. Unless I decide for him, his fires will scorch me up."

While we were thus discussing the subject of the god of Love, a slave of Charicles suddenly rushed in bearing his evil tidings on his face so plainly, that Clinias immediately cried out, "Some accident has befallen Charicles." "Charicles," hastily exclaimed the slave, "is dead." Utterance failed Clinias, upon hearing this, he remained without the power of motion, as if struck by lightning. The slave proceeded to relate the sad particulars. "Charicles," he said, "after mounting, went off at a moderate pace, then after having had two or three gallops, pulled up, and still sitting on the animal, wiped off from its back the sweat, leaving the reins upon its neck. There was a sudden noise from behind, and the startled horse rearing bounded forward and dashed wildly on. Taking the bit between his teeth, with neck thrown up and tossing mane, maddened with fright, he flew through the air. Such was his speed, that his hind feet seemed endeavouring to overtake and pass the fore feet in the race; and owing to this rivalry of speed between the legs, the animal's back rose and fell as does a ship when tossing upon the billows. Oscillating from the effect of these wave-like movements, the wretched Charicles was tossed up and down like a ball upon the horse's back, now thrown back upon his croup, now pitched forward upon his neck. At length overmastered by the storm, and unable to recover possession of the reins, he gave himself up to this whirlwind of speed, and was at Fortune's mercy. The horse still in full career, turned from the public road, made for a wood, and dashed his unhappy rider against a tree. Charicles was shot from off his back as from an engine, and his face encountering the boughs, was lacerated with a wound from every jagged point. Entangled by the reins, he was unable to release his body, but was dragged along upon the road to death; for the horse, yet more affrighted by the rider's fall, and impeded by his body, kicked and trampled the miserable youth who was the obstacle to his farther flight; and such is his disfigurement that you can no longer recognize his features."

After listening to this account, Clinias was for some moments speechless through bewilderment, then awakening from his trance of grief, he uttered a piercing cry, and was rushing out to meet the corpse, I following and doing my best to comfort him. At this instant the body of Charicles was borne into the house, a wretched and pitiable sight, for he was one mass of wounds, so that none of the bystanders could restrain their tears. His father led the strains of lamentation, and cried out, "My son, in how different a state hast thou returned from that in which thou didst leave me! Ill betide all horsemanship! Neither hast thou died by any common death, nor art thou brought back a corpse comely in thy death; others who die preserve their well-known lineaments, and though the living beauty of the countenance be gone, the image is preserved, which by its mimickry of sleep consoles the mourner. In their case, death has taken away the soul, but leaves in the body the semblance of the individual: in thy case, fate has destroyed both, and, to me, thou hast died a double death, in soul and body, so utterly has even the shadow of thy likeness perished! Thy soul has fled, and I find thee no more, even in body! Oh, my son, when shall be now thy bridal day? When, ill-starred horseman and unwedded bridegroom, when shall be the joyous nuptial festivities? The tomb will be thy bridal bed, death thy partner, a dirge thy nuptial song, wailing thy strains of joy! I thought, my son, to have kindled for thee a very different flame, but cruel fate has extinguished both it and thee, and in its stead lights up the funeral torch. Oh, luckless torch bearing, where death presides and takes the place of marriage!"

Thus bitterly did the father bewail the loss of his son, and Clinias vied with him in the expression of his grief, breaking forth into soliloquy. "I have been the death of him who was master of my affection! Why was I so ill-advised as to present him with such a gift! Could I not have given him a golden beaker, out of which, when pouring a libation, he might have drunk, and so have derived pleasure from the gift? Instead of doing this, wretch that I was, I bestowed upon this beauteous youth a savage brute, and moreover decked out the beast with a pectoral and frontlet and silver trappings. Yes, Charicles, I decked out your murderer with gold! Thou beast, of all others most evil, ruthless, ungrateful, and insensible to beauty, thou hast actually been the death of him who fondled thee, who wiped away thy sweat, promised thee many a feed, and praised the swiftness of thy pace! Instead of glorying in being the bearer of so fair a youth, thou hast ungratefully dashed his beauty to the earth! Woe is me, for having bought this homicide, who has turned out to be thy murderer!"

No sooner were the funeral obsequies over, than I hastened to the maiden, who was in the pleasance belonging to the house. It consisted of a grove, which afforded a delightful object to the eyes; around it ran a wall, each of the four sides of which had a colonnade supported upon pillars, the central space being planted with trees, whose branches were so closely interwoven, that the fruits and foliage intermingled in friendly union. Close to some of the larger trees grew the ivy and the convolvulus; the latter hanging from the plane-trees, clustered round it, with its delicate foliage; the former twining round the pine, lovingly embraced its trunk, so that the tree became the prop of the ivy, and the ivy furnished a crown for the tree. On either side were seen luxuriant vines, supported upon reeds; these were now in blossom, and hanging down from the intervening spaces were the ringlets of the plant; while the upper leaves, agitated by the breeze and interpenetrated by the rays of the sun, caused a quivering gleam to fall upon the ground, which partially lighted up its shade. Flowers also displayed the beauty of their various hues. The narcissus, the rose, and violet, mingling together, imparted a purple colour to the earth; the calyx of both these flowers was alike in its general shape, and served them for a cup; the expanded rose-leaves were red and violet above, milky white below, and the narcissus was altogether of the latter hue; the violet had no calyx, and its colour resembled that of the sea when under the influence of a calm. In the midst of the flowers bubbled a fountain, whose waters received into a square basin, the work of art, served the flowers for their mirror, and gave a double appearance to the grove, by adding the reflection to the reality. Neither were there wanting birds: some of a domestic kind, reared by the care of man, were feeding in the grove; while others, enjoying their liberty of wing, flew and disported themselves among the branches. The songsters were grasshoppers and swallows, of which the one celebrated the rising of Aurora, the other the banquet of Tereus. Those of a domestic kind were the peacock, the swan, and the parrot; the swan was feeding near the fountain; a cage suspended from a tree contained the parrot; the peacock drew after him his splendid train; nor was it easy to decide which surpassed the other in beauty, the tints of the flowers themselves, or the hues of his flower-like feathers.

Leucippe happened at this time to be walking with Clio, and stopped opposite the peacock who was just then spreading his train, and displaying the gorgeous semicircle of his feathers. Wishing to produce amorous sensations in her mind, I addressed myself to the slave Satyrus, making the peacock the subject of our discourse. "The bird," I said, "does not do this without design; he is of an amorous nature, and always bedecks himself in this manner when he wishes to attract his favourite mate. Do you see," I added, (pointing in the direction) "the female, near the plane-tree yonder? It is to her that he is now displaying the 'enamelled meadow' of his plumes, and this meadow of his is assuredly more beautiful than any mead in nature, each plume has in it a spot of gold, and the gold is encircled by a purple ring, and so in every plume there is seen an eye." Satyrus readily comprehended the drift of my discourse, and in order to give me scope for continuing the subject, he asked "whether Love could possibly possess such power as to transmit his warmth even unto the winged tribes?" "Yes," I replied, "not only unto them—for there is no marvel in this, since he himself is winged— but also into reptiles and wild beasts and plants; nay, in my opinion even unto stones. The magnet, for instance loves the iron, and upon the first sight and touch draws that metal towards it, as if containing within itself the fire of love. Is there not in this, a manifest embrace between the amorous stone and the iron the object of its affection? Philosophers, moreover, tell, concerning plants, what I should deem an idle tale were it not confirmed by the experience of husbandmen. They maintain that one plant becomes enamoured of another, and that the palm is most sensible of the tender passion; there are, you must know, male and female palms; supposing the female is planted at a distance from it, the male droops and withers; the husbandman upon seeing this, easily understands the nature of the malady, and ascending an eminence he observes in what direction the tree inclines—which is always towards the beloved object; having ascertained this point, he employs the following remedy: taking a shoot from the female he inserts it into the very heart of the male; this immediately revives it, and bestows new life upon its sinking frame, so that it recovers its pristine vigour; and this arises from delight in embracing its beloved; such are the loves of the plants.

"The same holds true concerning streams and rivers also; for we hear of the loves of the river Alpheus and the Sicilian fountain Arethusa. This river takes its course through the sea as through a plain, and the sea instead of impregnating it with its saltness, divides and so affords a passage for the river, performing the part of bridesman, by conducting it to Arethusa; when, therefore, at the Olympic Festival, persons cast various gifts into the channel of this river, it immediately bears them to its beloved, these being its nuptial gifts. A yet stranger mystery of Love is seen in reptiles, not merely in those of like race, but of different kind. The viper conceives a violent passion for the lamprey, which though in form a serpent, is to all intents and purposes a fish. When these reptiles wish to copulate, the viper goes down to the shore and hisses in the direction of the sea, which is a signal to the lamprey; she understands the sound, and issues from the water, but does not immediately hasten to her lover, knowing that he carries deadly poison in his teeth, but gliding up a rock, there waits until he has cleansed his mouth. After looking at one another for a space, the loving viper vomits forth the poison so dreaded by his mistress, and she upon perceiving this, descends and entwines him in her embrace, no longer dreading his amorous bite."

During my discourse, I kept observing Leucippe to see how she took these amatory topics, and she gave indications that they were not displeasing to her. The dazzling beauty of the peacock which I just now mentioned seemed to me far inferior to her attractions; indeed the beauty of her countenance might vie with the flowers of the meadow; the narcissus was resplendent in her general complexion, the rose blushed upon her cheek, the dark hue of the violet sparkled in her eyes, her ringlets curled more closely than do the clusters of the ivy;——her face, therefore, was a reflex of the meadows. Shortly after this, she left the pleasance, it being time for her to practise upon the harp. Though absent she appeared to me still present, for her form and features remained impressed upon my eyes.

Satyrus and I congratulated each other upon our mutual performances. I for the subjects I had chosen, he for having given me the opportunity of discussing them. Supper time soon arrived and we reclined at table as before.

Book II

Previous to this, however, Satyrus and I, praising our mutual tact, proceeded to the maiden's chamber, under the pretext of hearing her performance on the harp, but in reality because I could not bear her to be out of my sight, for however short a space. The first subject of her song was, the engagement between the lion and the boar, described by Homer; afterwards she chose a tenderer theme, the praises of the rose.

Divested of its poetic ornaments, the purport of the strain was this: Had Jove wished to impose a monarch upon the flowers, this honor would have been given to the rose, as being the ornament of the earth, the boast of shrubs, the eye of flowers, imparting a blush to the meadows and dazzling with its beauty. The rose breathes of love, conciliates Venus, glories in its fragrant leaves, exults in its tender stalks, which are gladdened by the Zephyr. Such was the matter of the song. For my part, I seemed to behold a rose upon her lips, as though the calyx of the flower had been converted into the form of the human mouth. She had scarcely ended when the supper hour arrived. It was then the time of celebrating the Festival of Bacchus, "patron of the vintage," whom the Tyrians esteem to be their god, quoting a legend of Cadmus which attributes to the feast the following origin:—Once upon a time, mortals had no such thing as wine, neither the black and fragrant kind, nor the Biblian, nor the Maronæan, nor the Chian, nor the Icarian; all these they maintain came originally from Tyre, their inventor being a Tyrian. A certain hospitable neatherd (resembling the Athenian Icarius, who is the subject of a very similar story) gave occasion to the legend which I am about to relate. Bacchus happened to come to the cottage of this countryman, who set before him whatsoever the earth and the labours of his oxen had produced. Wine, as I observed, was then unknown, like the oxen, therefore, their beverage was water.

Bacchus thanked him for his friendly treatment and presented to him a "loving cup," which was filled with wine. Having taken a hearty draught, and becoming very jovial from its effects, he said:—"Whence, stranger, did you procure this purple water, this delicious blood? It is quite different from that which flows along the ground; for that descends into the vitals, and affords cold comfort at the best; where as this, even before entering the mouth, rejoices the nostrils, and though cold to the touch, leaps down into the stomach and begets a pleasurable warmth."

To this Bacchus replied, "This is the water of an autumnal fruit, this is the blood of the grape," and so saying, he conducted the neatherd to a vine, and squeezing a bunch of grapes said, "here is the water, and this is the fountain from whence it flows." Such is the account which the Tyrians give as to the origin of wine.

It was, as I before said, the festival of this deity which was being celebrated. My father anxious to do everything handsomely, had made grand preparations for the supper, and there was set in honor of the god, a magnificent goblet of crystal, in the beauty of its workmanship second only to that of the Chian Glaucus. Vines seemingly growing from within encircled it, and their clusters hung down all around; as long as the goblet remained empty each grape appeared unripe and green; but no sooner was the wine poured in than each grape began to redden, and assumed the hue of ripeness; and among them was represented Bacchus himself as dresser of the vineyard. As the feast went on, and the good wine did its office, I began to cast bold lawless glances at Leucippe; for Love and Bacchus are two very potent deities, they take possession of the soul and so inflame it that it forgets every restraint of modesty; the one kindles in it a flame, and the other supplies fuel for the fire, for wine may truly be called the meat and drink of love. The maiden also became gradually emboldened so as to gaze at me more fixedly. In this manner, ten days passed on without anything beyond glances being interchanged between us.

At length I imparted the whole affair to Satyrus, requesting his assistance; he replied, "I knew it all before you told me, but was unwilling that you should be aware of the fact, supposing it your wish to remain unobserved; for very often he who loves by stealth hates the party who has discovered his passion, and considers himself to have received an insult from him. However," continued he, "fortune has provided for our contingences, for Clio, Leucippe's chambermaid, has an understanding with me, and admits me as her lover. I will gradually buy her over to give us her assistance in this affair; but you, on your part, must not be content with making trial of the maiden merely by glances; you must speak to her and say something to the point, then take a farther step by touching her hand, squeezing her fingers, and fetching a deep sigh; if she permits this willingly, then salute her as the mistress of your affections, and imprint a kiss upon her neck." "By Pallas, you counsel wisely," was my reply, "but I fear me, I shall prove but a craven wrestler in the school of love."

"The god of love," said he, "has no notion of craven-heartedness; do you not see in what warlike guise he is equipped? He bears a bow, a quiver, arrows, and a lighted torch, emblems all of them, of manhood and of daring. Filled, then, as you are with the influence of such a god, are you a coward and do you tremble? Beware of shewing yourself merely a counterfeit in love. I will make an opening by calling away Clio, as soon as an opportunity occurs for your having a private conversation with Leucippe." With these words he left the room; excited by what he had said, I was no sooner alone, then I used every endeavour to collect my courage for the approaching interview. "Coward," said I, "how long wilt thou continue silent? Thou, the soldier of such a warlike 'god, and yet a craven.' Dost thou intend to wait until the maiden comes to thee of her own accord?" Afterwards I proceeded, "and yet fool that thou art, why not come to thy senses? Why not bestow thy love upon a lawful object? Thou hast another maiden in this house; one possessed of beauty. Be content with loving *her*, and gazing upon *her*; her it is permitted thee to take to wife." My purpose was almost fixed; when from the bottom of my heart Love spoke in reply and said; "Rash man, darest thou to set thyself in array and to war with me—me, who have wings to fly, arrows to wound, and a torch to burn? How, prythee, wilt thou escape? If thou wardest off my shafts, how wilt thou avert my fire? and even supposing thy chastity should quench the flame, still I can overtake thee with my wings."

While engaged in this soliloquy, the maiden unexpectedly made her appearance; I turned pale, and the next moment became crimson; she was quite alone, not even Clio accompanied her; in a very confused manner, and not knowing what else to say, I addressed her with the words, "Good morrow, fair mistress;" sweetly smiling, she shewed by her countenance that she comprehended the drift of my salutation, and said, "Do you call me your mistress?" "Indeed I do, for one of the gods has told me to be your slave, as Hercules was sold to Omphale." "Sold, if I remember, by Mercury," rejoined she, "and Jove employed him in the business;" this she said with an arch smile. "What nonsense," rejoined I, "to trifle so, and talk of Mercury when all the while you understood my meaning." While one pleasantry led on to another and so prolonged our conversation, fortune came to my assistance.

About noon on the preceding day, Leucippe had been playing on the harp and Clio was sitting beside her. I was walking up and down, when suddenly a bee flying in, stung Clio's hand; she immediately shrieked out, upon which the maiden, hastily rising from her seat and laying aside the harp, examined the wound, bidding her to be under no anxiety, for that she could relieve the pain by simply uttering two magic words, having been instructed by an Egyptian how to cure the stings inflicted by bees and wasps; she then proceeded to utter the words of incantation, and Clio, in a few moments declared the pain to be relieved. This, as I intimated, took place on the day before. On the present occasion it chanced, that a bee or wasp flew buzzing round my face, when all at once the idea seized me of feigning myself to have been stung; I did so, putting my hand to my face, and pretending to be in pain. The maiden came up to me, removed my hand and enquired where I had been stung; upon my lips, dearest, was my reply, why do you not charm away the pain? Approaching my face, she placed her mouth almost close to mine, in order to work the charm, at the same time murmuring certain words, and ever and anon touching my lips. All this time I kept stealing silent kisses, so that from the maiden alternately opening and closing her lips while uttering the charm, the incantation became changed into one continuous kiss. At last putting my arms around her, I saluted her lips more ardently; upon which drawing back she exclaimed, "What are you about? Are you, too, turned enchanter?" "I am only kissing the charm which has removed my pain." She took my meaning and smiled, which gave me a fresh supply of courage.

"Ah! dear Leucippe," I exclaimed, "I now feel another and severer sting, one which has penetrated to my very heart, and calls for your 'mighty magic;' surely you must carry about a bee upon your lips, they are full of honey, your kisses wound; repeat the charm, I pray, but do not worry over the operation, for fear of exasperating the wound;" at the same time I embraced her more closely and kissed her with still greater freedom; nor, though making a show of resistance, did she seem displeased. At this juncture Clio was seen approaching from a distance, upon which we separated, I much annoyed and sorely against my will; what were her feelings I cannot exactly say. After what had passed, however, I felt easier in mind and began to indulge in brighter hopes.

I still felt the kiss upon my lips as though it had really been something of a corporeal nature; I zealously guarded it as a treasure of sweets, for a kiss is to the lover his chief delight; it takes its birth from the fairest portion of the human body—from the mouth, which is the instrument of the voice, and the voice is the adumbration of the soul; when lips mingle they dart pleasure through the veins, and make even the lovers' souls join in the embrace. Never before did I feel delight comparable to this; and then for the first time I learnt that no pleasurable sensation can vie with a lover's kiss.

At supper time we met as on former occasions, when Satyrus, who acted as cupbearer, hit upon the following amorous device. After our cups were filled, he effected an exchange, presenting mine to the maiden, handing hers to me. Having noticed what part of the brim had been touched by her in drinking, I applied my lips to the same place; thus intimating that I was sending her a kiss. She remarked what I had done, and readily understood that I had been kissing the shadow of her lips. Satyrus again stealthily made a like exchange of cups, when I could observe her imitating me, and drinking as I had done, which, as you may imagine, vastly increased my happiness. This was repeated a third and fourth time; in short, we passed the rest of the time in drinking kisses to one another.

When supper was ended, Satyrus approaching me said, "Now is the time to show your mettle; the maiden's mother, as you are aware, is unwell, and has retired to rest alone. She herself before going to bed will take a few turns as usual in the garden, attended by no one but Clio, whom I will undertake to get out of the way." We then separated, and remained on the watch, he for Clio, I for Leucippe. Everything turned out as we had wished; Clio was got rid of, and Leucippe remained walking by herself. I waited till the daylight had faded away, and then approached her, emboldened by my former success, like a soldier already victorious, who therefore scorns the perils of war. The arms in which I trusted were wine, love, hope, and solitude; so, without saying a word, and as if everything had been preconcerted, I took her in my arms, and covered her with kisses. When about to proceed to other familiarities, a noise was heard behind us, at which we started asunder in alarm. She betook herself to her chamber, and I remained there in great dudgeon at having lost so capital an opportunity, and execrating the noise which had been the cause.

Meanwhile Satyrus came up with a laughing countenance. He had witnessed everything, having concealed himself under a tree to guard against our surprise; and it was he, who seeing some one approach, had made the noise.

In the course of a few days, my father made preparations for concluding my marriage sooner than had been originally intended. He had been much alarmed by various dreams; he thought he was celebrating the nuptial rites, and after the torches had been kindled the light was suddenly extinguished. This made him more anxious to conclude the matter, and we were now within a day of the one formally appointed for the ceremony. The wedding clothes and jewels were already purchased; there was a necklace composed of various gems, and a splendid purple robe edged with a gold border. The gems vied with each other in beauty; among them was a hyacinth, which resembled a rose, only that it was a stone, and an amethyst almost as lustrous as gold itself. In the middle of this necklace were three precious stones, arranged together and curiously blended in their hues; the lowest one was black, the middle white, but with a darkish tinge, the upper one shading off into a ruddy colour. They were set in a rim of gold, and might be said to bear resemblance to an eye. The purple of the dress was of no ordinary dye, but of the kind which the Tyrians fable to have been discovered by the shepherd's dog, and with which they are wont to represent the robe of Venus to be tinged. There was a time when this purple dye was as yet unknown, but remained concealed in the hollow of a little shell fish. A shepherd meeting with one of these hoped to obtain the fish which was inside; foiled by the hardness of the shell, after bestowing a hearty curse upon his booty, he threw it into the sea as so much worthless rubbish. His dog lighted upon this windfall, and broke open the shell with his teeth, in doing which his mouth and lips became stained with the brilliant dye, or as we may call it, blood. The shepherd upon seeing this supposed it the effect of a wound; so taking the dog down to the sea he washed his mouth, upon which the imaginary blood assumed a still more brilliant hue, and upon proceeding to touch it, his hand became of a purple colour. The shepherd now guessed what was the nature of the shell fish, and that it was impregnated with a dye of surpassing beauty; so taking some wool he placed it in the aperture, determined to dive into the mysteries of the shell; and it became of a colour similar to that upon the dog's mouth. By this means he obtained a knowledge of what we call purple; and after breaking open its fortified receptacle with the help of a stone, he arrived at the treasure-house of dye. To return, however, to my story. My father was performing the preliminary rites, the marriage being fixed, as I have said, for the following day. I was in despair, and was devising some pretext for deferring it. While in this state of perplexity, a great tumult was heard to proceed from the men's quarter of the house. It appeared that as my father was offering up a sacrifice; an eagle swooping from on high seized the victim, and in spite of every endeavour to scare him away, bore off his prey. As this was declared to forebode no good, the marriage was postponed for another day. My father proceeded to consult the seers and soothsayers upon the meaning of the portent; they were of opinion that he should offer a sacrifice to hospitable Jove at midnight upon the sea-shore, since the bird had flown in that direction. Sure enough he had winged his flight thither, and appeared no more. For my part, I extolled the eagle to the skies, and declared that he was justly styled the king of birds. No long time elapsed before the meaning of the prodigy became revealed. There was a certain young man, a native of Byzantium, by name Callisthenes; he was an orphan and possessed of wealth, profligate in his life and extravagant in his expenditure. Having heard that Sostratus had a handsome daughter, he was anxious to obtain her hand and became enamoured upon hearsay, for he had never seen her. The force of passion upon the licentious is often so strong that their ears lead them into love, and report has the same effect upon their minds which sight has upon others.

Before the breaking out of the war against the Byzantians, the young man introduced himself to Sostratus, and asked the hand of his daughter in marriage. Sostratus, however, strongly objecting to his irregular way of life, rejected his application. Callisthenes was very indignant at this repulse; he considered himself slighted;—besides, he was in love, and fancy pictured to his mind those charms which he had never seen. Dissembling his displeasure, he meditated how he might revenge himself on Sostratus, and at the same time gratify his own desires; nor was he without hope of success, there being a law of the Byzantians which enacted, that if any one should carry off a maiden he should be exempt from punishment upon making her his wife; of this law he determined to avail himself, and waited only till a seasonable opportunity should offer. Although the war had now broken out, and the maiden had come to us for security, he did not abandon his design, in the execution of which the following circumstance assisted, as the Byzantians had received an oracle to this effect:—

> "*With* plant-born *name there lives an island race,*
> *Whose land an isthmus to the shore doth brace;*
> *Vulcan consorts there with the blue-eyed maid,*
> *And there to Hercules be offerings paid.*"

While all were in doubt what place was intended by these enigmatic words, Sostratus (who was one of the commanders) thus delivered his opinion:—"We must send to Tyre, and offer up a sacrifice to Hercules; the expressions of the miracle clearly point to that city. The 'plant-derived name,' shews that the island of the Phœnicians is intended, the phœnix (or palm), being a plant; both sea and land lay claim to it: the latter joins it to the continent, the former washes it on either side; thus it is seated in the one element, but without abandoning the other, to which it is united by its narrow isthmus or neck of land; moreover, it is not founded in the sea, but both under it and under the isthmus, the waters have free course; thus there is seen the singular spectacle of a city in the sea, and of an island upon shore. The mention made of 'Vulcan consorting with the blue-eyed maid,' alludes to the olive and the fire, which are found there in close proximity: for, in a sacred precinct surrounded by a wall, olive trees are seen to flourish, while fire issuing from their roots burns among the branches, and with its ashes benefits the tree; hence there exists a mutual friendship, and Minerva shuns not Vulcan." Upon this Chærophon, who shared the command with Sostratus in the war, his senior in age and a native of Tyre, extolled him highly for his excellent interpretation of the oracle. "It is not only fire, however," said he, "which claims our wonder; the water also deserves its share. I myself have seen the following marvels:—there is a fountain in Sicily whose waters are mingled with fire; the flame is seen to leap up from underneath, yet if you touch the water it will be found as cold as snow, so that neither is the fire extinguished by the water, nor the water ignited by the flame, but a mutual truce subsists between the elements. There is also a river in Spain, not differing from others in appearance, but if you wish to hear it become vocal, you have but to wait and listen; for when a gentle breeze sweeps over its surface there is heard a sound as if from strings, the wind being the plectrum, the river itself the lyre. I may likewise mention a lake in Lybia, resembling in its nature the Indian soil. The Lybian maidens are well acquainted with its secrets and with the riches which, stored below its waters, are mingled with the mud, for it is, in fact, a fount of gold. Plunging a long pole smeared with pitch into the lake, they lay open its recesses; this pole is to the gold what the hook is to the fish, serving as a bait. The grains of gold alone attach themselves to the pitch, and are drawn on shore. Such is the gold-fishing in the Lybian waters."

After relating these marvels, Chærophon, with the consent of the state, proceeded to dispatch the victims and other offerings to Tyre. Callisthenes contrived to be among the number of the sacred functionaries, and soon arriving at that city, he found out my father's residence, and matured his schemes against the females, who, as will presently be shown, went out to view the sacrificial show, which was in the highest degree sumptuous; there was a vast quantity of different kinds of incense used, such as cassia, frankincense, and crocus; there was also a great display of flowers, the narcissus, the rose, and the myrtle; the fragrance of the flowers vied with the perfumes of the incense; the breeze wafted them aloft, mingled their odours in the air, producing a gale of sweets. The victims were many in number and of various kinds; the most remarkable among them, however, were the oxen from the Nile, animals which excel not only in stature but in colours. They are altogether of very large size, with brawny necks, broad backs, and ample bellies; their horns are not depressed, like those of the Sicilian ox, nor ill-shaped like the Cyprian, but project upward from the forehead of this animal with a gentle curve; the interval between them at their tips and at the roots being equal, so that they bear a resemblance to the moon when at the full; their colour is that which Homer so much praises in the Thracian horses. The bull stalks along with lofty crest, as if to show that he is the monarch of the herd. If there is any truth in the legend of Europa, it was into an Egyptian bull that Jove metamorphosed himself.

At the time of which I am speaking my mother-in-law was unwell; Leucippe also feigned indisposition, according to a preconcerted arrangement, that we might have an opportunity of meeting during the absence of the rest. My sister, therefore, and Leucippe's mother were the only ones who went out to see the show. Callisthenes, who knew by sight the wife of Sostratus, seeing my sister in her company mistook her for Leucippe, of whom he had no personal knowledge. Smitten by her appearance, and without making any inquiries, he points her out to a trusty attendant of his, commanding him to engage some pirates to effect her seizure, and arranging the manner of proceeding, for a high festival was at hand when, as he understood, all the maidens would go down to the shore for the purpose of performing their ablutions. After giving these directions, and having discharged the duties of his function, he withdrew. He had previously, I may remark, provided a vessel of his own, in case an opportunity should offer for carrying his schemes into effect.

Meanwhile the rest of the sacred functionaries had embarked and sailed away; he, however, went on board his vessel, and continued to lie a little off shore, both in order that he might appear to be taking his departure like the others, and also lest, being so near Tyre, any danger should happen to himself in consequence of carrying off the maiden. Upon arriving at Sarepta, a Tyrian village on the sea-coast, he purchased another craft, which he intrusted to his follower Zeno, who was to execute his plan. This man was able-bodied, and accustomed to a buccaneering life; he soon, therefore, succeeded in gathering together some pirates from the above-named village, and then sailed for Tyre. Near this city there is an islet with a harbour, (the Tyrians call it the tomb of Rhodope); here the craft was stationed watching for the prey. Before the arrival of the high festival, however, which Callisthenes awaited, the omen of the eagle and the interpretation of the soothsayers were fulfilled. On the day preceding, we made preparations for the sacrifice to Jove, and late in the evening went down to the shore; none of our motions escaped Zeno, who cautiously followed us. When in the act of performing our ablutions, he made the preconcerted signal, upon which the boat made rapidly for the land, manned by ten young fellows; eight others were secretly in readiness on shore, dressed in women's clothes and with shaven chins; each had a sword concealed under his dress, and the better to avoid any suspicion, they had brought some victims with them as for sacrifice, so that we took them to be women. No sooner had we reached the pile than, raising a sudden shout, they rushed upon us, and put out our torches; we fled disorderly and in alarm, upon which they drew their swords, and seizing my sister, put her into the boat, and then embarking rowed off with the speed of an eagle. Some who had fled at the first onset saw nothing of what afterwards occurred; others who had witnessed everything cried out, "The pirates have carried off Calligone."

Meanwhile the boat was far out at sea, and upon nearing Sarepta made a signal which when Callisthenes recognised, he put out to meet it, and taking the maiden on board his own vessel, at once sailed away. I breathed again upon finding my marriage thus unexpectedly broken off, nevertheless I was sorry for the calamity which had befallen my sister. A few days after this occurrence, I said to Leucippe, "How long, my dearest, are we to confine ourselves to kisses? they are pleasant enough as preludes, let us now add to them something more substantial; suppose we exchange mutual pledges of fidelity, for only let Venus initiate us in her mysteries and then we need fear the power of no other deity."

By constantly repeating my solicitations, I at length persuaded the maiden to receive me into her own chamber, Clio lending us her assistance. I will describe the situation of her room: a large space in one part of the mansion contained two chambers on the right hand and as many on the left; a narrow passage, closed at the entrance by a door, gave access to them. Those at the farther end were occupied by the maiden and her mother, and were opposite each other; of the two remaining ones, that next to Leucippe belonged to Clio, the other was a store-room. Leucippe's mother was always in the habit of attending her to bed; upon which occasions she not only locked the door inside, but had it secured by a slave on the outside, the keys being handed to her through an opening; these she kept until the morning, when calling the man she passed them back to him that he might unlock the door.

Satyrus contrived to have a set of keys made like them, and finding upon trial that they would answer, he with the consent of the maiden gained over Clio, who was to offer no impediment. Such was the plan which we devised. There was a slave belonging to the household, called Conops, a prying, talkative, lecherous fellow, in short everything that was bad. The man watched our proceedings very narrowly, and suspecting our intentions, used to keep open the door of his dormitory until late at night, so that it was no easy matter to escape his observation. Satyrus wishing to make a friend of him, often talked and joked with him, and laughing in allusion to his name (Κώνωψ) would call him Gnat. The fellow seeing through the artifice of Satyrus pretended to return the joke, but, in doing so, exhibited his own ill-natured disposition. "As you are so fond," said he, "of punning upon my name, I will tell you a story about the gnat. The lion often complained to Prometheus that although he had formed him a large and handsome beast, had armed his jaws with teeth, and his feet with claws, and had made him more powerful than the other animals, still, notwithstanding all these advantages, he stood in fear of the dunghill cock. 'Why dost thou without cause accuse me?' replied Prometheus; 'I have given thee every gift which it was in my power to bestow, it is thine own faint heartedness which is in fault.' The lion wept and bemoaned his condition, cursing his own want of courage, and in the end made up his mind to die. While in this frame of mind he happened to meet the elephant, with whom, after wishing him good morning, he entered into conversation. Seeing him continually flap his ears, 'What ails you,' he asked—'why are your ears never for a moment still?' The elephant, about whose head a gnat was at that moment flying, replied, 'If the buzzing insect which I see, was to get into my ear, the result would be my death.' Upon this the lion made the following reflection. 'Why should I (such as I am, and so much more fortunate than the elephant,) think of dying? It is better to stand in awe of a cock than to dread a scurvy gnat.'

"You see," said Conops, "what power the gnat possesses, since he can terrify the elephant." Satyrus who saw into the malicious meaning of his words, replied with a smile, "I will now relate to you the story of the gnat and the lion, which I heard from a certain sage; as for your tale about the elephant, you are welcome to make what you can out of it. The braggart gnat said one day to the lion, 'So you think to lord it over me as you do over other creatures. I should like to know why? You are not handsomer than I am, nor yet bolder, nor yet more powerful; in what respect are you superior to me? In valour?—You tear with your claws and bite with your teeth, it is true; so does every woman when she quarrels; and as to your size and beauty, you have indeed an ample chest and broad shoulders, and a whole forest of hair about your neck, but you little think how unsightly are your hinder parts. On the other hand, my greatness is commensurate with the air and with the power of my wings; the flowers of the meadow constitute my comeliness, they serve me in lieu of garments, with which, when weary with flying, I invest myself; neither is my valour any laughing matter; I am the very impersonation of a warlike instrument; I blow a blast when I go to battle, and it is my mouth which serves for trumpet and for weapon, so that I am at once, a musician and an archer; moreover I am my own bow and arrow; my wings poised in air shoot me forward, and lighting down, I inflict a wound as with a shaft; who so ever feels it cries out and forthwith tries to find his enemy: I, however, though present, am at the same time absent; I fly and I stand my ground, and with my wings circle round the adversary, and laugh to see him dance with pain. But why should I waste more words?—let us at once join battle.' Saying this, he falls upon the lion, attacking his eyes and every other part which was unprotected by hair; at the same time wheeling round him and blowing his trumpet. The lion was in a fury, turning himself in every direction and vainly snapping at the air; his wrath afforded additional sport to the gnat, who made an onslaught on his very mouth. Immediately he turned to the side where he was aggrieved, when his antagonist, like a skilful wrestler, twisting and twirling his body escaped clean through the lion's teeth, which were heard to rattle against each other in the vain attempt to seize him. By this time the lion was thoroughly tired by thus fighting with the air, and stood still, exhausted by his own efforts; upon which the gnat, sailing round his mane sounded a triumphant strain of victory; but stimulated by his excess of vanity he took a wider range, and all at once fell into a spider's web. When no hope of escape appeared, he sorrowfully said, 'Fool that I am, I entered the lists against a lion, and behold I am caught in the meshes of a spider!'" Having finished his story, Satyrus said, with a sarcastic laugh, "Be on your guard, and beware of spiders." Not many days had passed when Satyrus knowing what a belly-slave Conops was, purchased a powerful soporific draught and then invited him to supper. Suspicious of some trick, he at first declined, but afterwards, over persuaded by his most excellent adviser—appetite, he complied. After supper, when he was on the point of going away, Satyrus poured the potion into his last draught, he drank it off, and had just time to reach his dormitory, when he fell on his bed in a deep sleep. Upon this, Satyrus hurried to me and said, "Conops is fast asleep, now is the time to prove yourself as valorous as Ulysses:" we instantly proceeded to the door which conducted to Leucippe's chamber; there he left me, and Clio stealthily admitted me, trembling with joy and fear; the dread of danger disturbed my hopes, but the hope of success qualified the dread, and so hope became the source of fear, and pain the cause of pleasure.

Just as I had entered the maiden's room, her mother's sleep had been disturbed by a fearful dream; a robber armed with a naked sword, seized and carried off her daughter, after which, laying her upon the ground, he proceeded to rip her up, beginning at her private parts. Terrified by the vision, her mother started up and hurried to her daughter's apartment, which as I before said was close at hand. I had but just got into bed and hearing the doors open, had scarcely time to leap out before she was at her daughter's side. Aware of my danger I made a bolt through the opened door, and ran with all my might, till trembling from head to foot I met Satyrus, when we both made our way in the dark and retreated each to his own room. Leucippe's mother fainted, but upon recovering the first thing she did was to box Clio's ears, then tearing her own hair, she broke forth into lamentation. "Oh Leucippe," she said, "you have blighted all my hopes. And you Sostratus, who are fighting at Byzantium to protect the honour of other people's wives and daughters, you little think how some enemy has been warring against your house, and has defiled your own daughter's honour. Oh, Leucippe, I never thought to see you wedded after such a fashion as this! Would that you had remained at Byzantium! Would that you had suffered violence from the chances of war, and that some Thracian had been your ravisher! In such a case the violence would have excused the shame, whereas now, you are at the same time wretched and disgraced. The vision of the night did but mock my mind, the realities of the dream were hidden from me, for of a truth, yours has been a more fearful ripping up, and your wound more fatal than any inflicted by the sword; and the worst is, that I am ignorant who is your ravisher. I do not even know what is his condition! for aught I can tell, he may be some wretched slave." When the maiden felt assured of my escape, she took courage and said: "Mother, there is no occasion for you to attack my chastity, nothing has been done to me deserving of your reproaches; nor do I know whether the intruder was a god, a demigod, or a mortal ravisher; all I know is that I was heartily frightened and lay still, quite unable to cry out through fear; for fear, as you know, acts as a padlock upon the tongue: this, however, you may be assured of, no one has robbed me of my virginity." Notwithstanding these assurances of her daughter, Panthea gave way to a fresh paroxysm of grief. Meanwhile Satyrus and I were deliberating on the best course to be pursued; and we determined to make our escape out of the house before morning should arrive, when Clio would be put to the torture and be compelled to reveal everything.

This plan we at once carried into execution, and telling the porter that we were going out to visit our mistresses, we went straight to Clinias: it was midnight, and we had some trouble in gaining admission: Clinias who slept in an upper room heard our voices in discussion with his porter, and hurried down in alarm, while we could see at a short distance Clio running towards us, for she too it appeared had determined to make her escape. Almost in the same moment therefore Clinias heard our story, and we the narrative of Clio, while she was made acquainted with our future plans; we all went in doors, when we gave Clinias a more detailed account and stated our determination of leaving the city. "I will accompany you," said Clio, "for if I remain behind till morning, death (the sweetest of torments, since it ends them) will be my lot." Clinias took my hand and leading me aside, he said, "It appears to me most advisable to get this wench out of the way at once, and after waiting a few days we can depart ourselves, if still of the same mind. According to your account the maiden's mother does not know who it was whom she surprised, nor will there be any one to furnish evidence since Clio is removed. Nay, we may perhaps persuade the maiden herself to share our flight; I will accompany you at all events."

We agreed to his proposal, so Clio was delivered to the care of one of his slaves to be put on board a boat, while we continued to deliberate upon the course best to be pursued. At last we resolved to make trial of Leucippe's inclination, and, should she be willing, to carry her off: in case of her rejecting our proposal, we determined to remain for the present and to await the course of events. The short remainder of the night was passed in sleep, and at daylight we returned home. Panthea had no sooner risen in the morning, than she had preparations made for putting Clio to the torture; but when summoned she could no where be found. Upon this, returning to her daughter, "Will you still persist," said she, "in concealing the particulars of this pretty plot? Now, I find that Clio also has run off." Still more reassured by the intelligence, Leucippe replied, "What more would you have me tell you? What stronger testimony of the truth would you have me produce? If there is any way of proving a maid's virginity, you are welcome to prove mine." "Aye," said Panthea, "and by so doing to add to the troubles of our family by bringing in witnesses to its disgrace;" upon saying which, she hastily quitted the apartment. Leucippe left to herself, and with her mother's words still ringing in her ears, was distracted by conflicting and various emotions; she was deeply pained at having been discovered. Her mother's reproaches filled her with shame; she felt angry at having her word doubted. Now these feelings are like three billows which disturb the soul's tranquillity: shame making an entrance through the eyes unfits them for their natural office; pain preys upon the mind and extinguishes its ardour; while the voice of anger baying round the heart overpowers reason with its wrathful foam. The tongue is the parent of these different feelings; bending its bow and aiming its arrow at the mark, it inflicts its several wounds upon the soul: with the wordy shaft of railing it produces anger, with that of well founded accusation, begets pain, with that of reproof, causes shame; the peculiarity of all these arrows is, that they inflict deep but bloodless wounds, and there is available against their effects one remedy alone, which is, to turn against the assailant his own weapons. Speech, the weapon of the tongue, must be repelled by a weapon of like nature, for then the feeling of anger will become calmed and the sensations of shame and annoyance will be appeased; but if dread of a superior hinder the employment of such succours, the very fact of silence makes these wounds to rankle the more deeply, and unless these mental waves, raised by the power of speech, can cast up their foam, they will but swell and toss the more.

What I have been saying will picture the condition of Leucippe's mind, who felt ready to sink under her troubles; it was while she was in this frame of mind that I dispatched Satyrus to her, in order to make overtures of flight. Anticipating him in her words, she exclaimed:—"In the name of the gods, foreign and hospitable, deliver me out of my mother's power, and take me whither you will; for if you go away and leave me here, the noose suspended by my own hands shall be my death." When I was informed of her expressions, it freed me from a world of anxiety; and in the course of two or three days, when my father was absent from home, we made preparations for our flight. Satyrus had still remaining some of the potion which he had used so successfully upon Conops. While waiting at supper he poured out a little into the last cup, which he presented to Panthea; almost immediately after drinking it, she retired to her own room, and fell fast asleep. Leucippe had now another chambermaid, with whom Satyrus was on familiar terms; having given her likewise a portion of the draught, he proceeded to a third party, the porter, who was soon lying under the influence of the same soporific potion.

Meanwhile Clinias was awaiting us at the door with a carriage which he had in readiness, and while all were yet asleep, between nine and ten at night, we cautiously left the house, Satyrus leading Leucippe by the hand: Conops, as I may remark, who used to watch our movements, being fortunately absent, having been dispatched on an errand by his mistress. On getting out, we immediately entered the carriage, six in number, Leucippe, I and Satyrus, together with Clinias and two servants. We drove off in the direction of Sidon, where we arrived about midnight, and without delay continued our journey to Berytus, in hopes of finding some vessel in the harbour; nor were we disappointed, for on going to the port we found a ship on the point of sailing: without even inquiring whither she was bound, we got our baggage on board, and embarked a little before dawn. It was then we learnt that the vessel was bound for the celebrated city of Alexandria, situated on the Nile.

The sight of the sea delighted me while as yet we were in the smooth water of the harbour; soon, however, upon the wind becoming favourable, loud tumult prevailed throughout the vessel; the sailors hurried to and fro, the master issued his commands, ropes were bent, the sail-yard was brought round before the wind, the sail was unfurled, we weighed anchor, the ship began to move, the port was left behind, and the coast, as if itself in motion, seemed gradually to be retiring from us; the Pæan was chanted, and many prayers were addressed to the guardian deities for a prosperous voyage. Meanwhile the wind freshened and filled the sail, and the vessel speeded on her course.

There was a young man on board, in the same cabin with ourselves, when dinner time was come he politely invited us to partake of his meal. Satyrus was just then bringing out our provisions; so putting all into a common stock, we shared our dinner and our conversation. I began by saying, "Pray where do you come from, and by what name are we to address you?" "My name," he replied, "is Menelaus, and I am a native of Egypt; and now may I inquire who you are?" "I am called Clitopho, and my companion Clinias; our country is Phœnicia." "And what," he rejoined, "is the motive of your voyage?" "If you will relate your own story first, you shall then hear ours." Menelaus assented, and began as follows:—

"The cause of my leaving my home may be summed up in very few words:—envious love and ill-fated hunting. I was strongly attached to a handsome youth, who was very fond of the chase. I did everything in my power to restrain him from this pursuit, but without success. Finding I could not prevail with him, I myself accompanied him.

"One day we were out hunting, and for a time everything went on successfully so long as harmless animals were alone the objects of our sport. At length a wild boar was roused; the youth pursued the brute, who faced about, and ran furiously to attack him; still the youth kept his ground, not withstanding that I repeatedly called out:—'Wheel round your horse; the beast is too powerful for you.' The boar continuing its career, and coming up, they closed in combat. Terrified lest the beast should wound the horse, and so bring down his rider, I launched my javelin without taking sufficient aim, and the youth crossing its course, received the stroke.

"Picture to yourself the feelings of my mind. If I retained life at that moment, it was like a living death; and what was most lamentable of all, the wretched youth, who still breathed, extending his arms, embraced me, and so far from hating his destroyer, he expired still grasping my homicidal hand. On account of this lamentable occurrence his parents took legal proceedings against me; nor was I unwilling to stand my trial; indeed I offered no defence, considering myself fully deserving to suffer death. The judge, out of compassion, condemned me to three years' banishment, and that period having now expired, I am on my return home."

This narrative reminded Clinias of the unhappy death of Charicles, and he shed tears, which though in appearance they flowed for another's grief, were, in reality, drawn forth by his own sorrows. "Are you weeping on my account," asked Menelaus, "or has any similar disaster befallen you?" Upon this Clinias, with many sighs, detailed the circumstances of Charicles and the horse; and I likewise related my adventures. Seeing Menelaus very low spirited on account of his own thoughts, and Clinias still shedding tears at the recollection of Charicles, I endeavoured to dissipate their grief, by introducing a love topic for conversation; for Leucippe, I may observe, was not then present, but was asleep in the ship's hold. I began, therefore, with a smiling air:—"How much better off is Clinias than I am; he was no doubt longing to inveigh against women, according to his wont, and he can do so all the better now, having found one who sympathises with his tastes; but why so many should be addicted to the love of youths, for my part I cannot tell."

"There can be no doubt," said Menelaus, "which is preferable. Youths are much more open and free from affectation than women, and their beauty stimulates the senses much more powerfully."

"How so?" I asked; "it no sooner appears than it is gone. It affords no enjoyment to the lover, but is like the cup of Tantalus, while one is drinking the liquid disappears; and even the little which has been swallowed is unsatisfying. No one can leave such favourites without feeling his pleasure alloyed with pain, the draught of love still leaves him thirsty."

"You do not understand," rejoined Menelaus, "that the perfection of pleasure consists in its bringing with it no satiety; the very fact of its being of a permanent and satisfying kind takes away from its delight. What we snatch but now and then is always new, and always in full beauty. Of such things the pleasure is not liable to decay and age, and it gains in intensity what it loses by briefness of duration; for this reason, the rose is considered the most lovely among flowers, because its beauty so quickly fades. There are two species of beauty among mortals, each bestowed by its presiding goddess; the one is of heaven, the other of earth; the former chafes at being linked to what is mortal, and quickly wings its flight to heaven; the latter clings to earth, and cleaves to mortal bodies. Would you have a poet's testimony of the ascent of heavenly beauty? hear what Homer sings:—

> 'Ganymede,
> *Fairest of human kind, whom for that cause*
> *The gods caught up to heav'n that he might dwell*
> *For ever there, the cup-bearer of Jove.'*

But no woman, I trow, ever ascended to heaven for her beauty's sake, though Jove had abundance of intrigues with women: grief and exile were the portion of Alcmena; the chest and the sea were the receptacle of Danæ; and Semele became food for fire; but—mark the difference—when Jove became enamoured of a Phrygian youth, he took him up to heaven to dwell with him, and pour out his nectar, depriving his predecessor of the office, she being, I rather think, a woman."

"In my opinion," said I, interrupting him, "female beauty has in it much more of the heavenly kind, because it does not so quickly fade; and the freer from decay, the nearer is anything to the divine nature. On the other hand, whatsoever in accordance with its mortal nature soon decays, is not of heaven, but of earth. I grant that Jove, enamoured of a Phrygian youth, raised him to the skies, but the beauty of woman brought him down from heaven; for a woman he bellowed under the form of a bull, for a woman he danced as a satyr, for a woman he transformed himself into a golden shower. Let Ganymede, therefore, be Jove's cup-bearer, if you will, provided that Juno also reclines at the banquet, and has a youth to wait on her. For my part, I cannot think upon his rape without feelings of pity: a savage bird is sent down, he is seized and borne aloft (cruel and tyrannous treatment, methinks), and the unseemly spectacle is seen of a youth suspended from an eagle's talons. No ravenous bird of prey, but the element of fire, bore Semele aloft; nor should there seem anything strange and unnatural in this, since it was by the same means that Hercules went up to heaven. You amuse yourself at the expense of Danæ's chest, but why do you pass over Perseus, who shared her fate? For Alcmena it sufficed that Jove for love of her robbed the world of three whole days.

"Passing, however, from the legends of mythology, I will speak of the real delights of love, though my experience in such matters has been small, compared with that of others, and confined to females who sell their charms for lucre. In the first place, how tender and yielding is a woman's body to the touch, how soft are her lips when kissed; her person is in every way fitted for the amorous embrace: he who is connected with her tastes genuine enjoyments; her kisses are impressed upon his lips as seals upon a letter, and she kisses with such studied art as imbues the kiss with double sweetness. Not content to use her lips, she brings her teeth also into play, and feeding upon her lover's mouth, makes her very kisses bite. What pleasure also is there in the sensation of pressing a woman's breast, while in the amorous crisis, so powerful is her excitement, that she is actually maddened with delight. Her kisses are not confined to the lips, but lovers' tongues even do their endeavour to kiss each other. At the conclusion of the amorous combat, she pants, overcome with the fiery delight, and her love-sick breath finding its way to her lips, encounter the lover's kiss still wandering there, and mingling with it both descend and exert their electric influence upon her heart, which leaps and beats, and were it not fast bound within, would desert its seat, and be drawn forth by the strength of kisses."

"Upon my word," said Menelaus, "you seem no raw recruit, but a thorough veteran in the service of the Queen of Love, so minute are you in all your detail. Now hear what I have to say in favour of male beauty. With women their words and postures, everything, in short, is studied and artificial: and their beauty, if they possess any, is the laborious work of cosmetic appliances, of perfumes and of dyes; divest them of these meretricious attractions, and they will appear like the daw stripped of its feathers, which we read of in the fable. The beauty of youths, on the other hand, requires no unguents or artificial essences to recommend it; nature has made it complete and sufficient in itself."

Book III

O n the third day of our voyage a sudden change took place in the weather; the sky, which had been clear, grew so black as quite to obscure the light of day, and a violent gale ploughing up the sea blew directly in our teeth. Upon this, the master ordered the yard to be brought round; the sailors speedily obeyed, furling one-half of the sail by dint of great exertions, but were compelled by the violence of the wind to leave the other unfurled. In consequence of this manœuvre one side of the vessel began to heel, while the contrary side became proportionally elevated, so that we every moment expected to be capsized, as the gale continued to blow with undiminished fury. To prevent this, and to restore, if possible, the vessel's equilibrium, we all scrambled to the side highest out of water, but it was of no avail. We ourselves, indeed, were raised, but the position of the ship was in no way altered; after long and vain endeavours to right her, the wind suddenly shifted, almost submerging the side which had been elevated, and raising high out of the water that previously depressed. An universal shriek arose from those on board, and nothing remained but to hurry back to our former station. We repeated this several times, our movements keeping pace with the shifting of the vessel; indeed, we had scarcely succeeded in hurrying to one side, before we were obliged to hurry back in the contrary direction. Like those who run backwards and forwards in the course, we continued these alternate movements during a great part of the day, momentarily expecting death, who, as it seemed, was not far off; for about noon the sun entirely disappeared, and we saw each other as if by moonlight; lightnings flashed from the clouds, the thunder rolled, filling the sky with its echoes, which were repeated from below by the strife of waters, while in the intermediate space was heard the shouts of the discordant winds, so that the air seemed one mighty trumpet; the ropes breaking loose rattled against the sail and against each other till at last they were rent in pieces. We now began to be in no small fear that the vessel, from the shattered condition of her sides, would open and go to pieces; the bulwarks too were flooded, being continually washed over by the waves. We however crawled under them for protection, and abandoning all hope resigned ourselves to Fortune. Tremendous billows following in quick succession tumbled one over the other, some in front, some at the sides of the ship, which as they approached was lifted high up as if upon a mountain, and when they retired was plunged down as into an abyss. The most formidable were those which broke against the sides and made their way over the bulwarks, flooding all the vessel; even while approaching from a distance these were formidable enough, almost touching, as they did, the clouds; but when they neared and broke, you would have supposed that the ship must inevitably be swallowed up. We could scarcely keep our feet, so violent was the rolling of the vessel, and a confused din of sounds was heard;—the sea roared, the wind blustered, the women shrieked, the men shouted, the sailors called to one another: all was wailing and lamentation.

At length the master ordered the cargo to be thrown overboard; no distinction was made between gold and silver, and the commonest articles,—all were pitched over the sides; many of the merchants with their own hands tumbling into the sea the goods on which all their hopes were centred. By these means the ship was lightened, but the storm did not in any degree abate. At length the master, wearied out and in despair, let go the tiller, abandoned the ship to the waves, and standing at the gangway ordered the boats to be got ready and the sailors to embark. Upon this a fearful scene of strife arose; the sailors in the boat were beginning to cut the rope which attached it to the ship. Seeing this, the passengers endeavoured to leap in, which the crew would not allow, threatening with their swords and axes any who should venture on the attempt. The others upon this arming themselves as best they could with shattered oars and broken benches, showed a determination to retaliate, for in a storm might, not right, must settle matters. A novel kind of sea-fight now commenced; they in the boat, fearful of being swamped by the numbers who were descending from the vessel, laid about them in good earnest with their swords and axes; which the passengers as they leaped in were not backward in returning with their poles and oars, and some scarcely touched the boat before they fell into the water; others, who had succeeded in getting in, were struggling with the sailors to maintain their ground. The laws of friendship or neighbourly regard were no longer heeded; each looked to his own preservation, careless of the safety of any other; for the effect of pressing danger is, that it dissolves even the tenderest ties. One of the passengers, a robust young fellow, succeeded at last in getting hold of the rope and dragging the boat towards the vessel; every one on board holding himself ready to leap in. A few succeeded in the endeavour, though not without receiving injuries; many in their attempt were plunged into the sea. The crew without further delay, cutting the rope with their axes, put off, and committed themselves to the mercy of the winds; those on board in the meantime having used every exertion to sink the boat. The vessel, after continuing for some time to pitch and roll upon the waves, was carried upon a sunken rock, when she struck and soon went to pieces, the mast falling over on one side and hastening her destruction. They who were at once swallowed up in the briny waves experienced a happier lot than their companions, in not having to remain with death before their eyes; for at sea the anticipation of drowning kills even before death actually arrives; the eye, bewildered by the expanse of waters, can set no limits to its fears: this it is which gives death so much more bitterness, and makes it regarded with dread proportioned to the vast nature of the sea itself.

Upon the present occasion some were dashed against rocks and perished, others were pierced by pieces of broken oars, and some were seen swimming in a half-exhausted state. When the vessel was wrecked, some good genius preserved a portion of the prow, upon which I and Leucippe being seated, were carried along by the current; Menelaus, Satyrus, and some other passengers, had thrown themselves across the mast; Clinias at no great distance was swimming supported by the yard, and we could hear him calling out, "Hold on, Clitopho!" In a moment a wave washed over him; at which sad spectacle we shrieked aloud. Boiling onward in our direction, it happily passed us, and we again caught sight of the yard, and Clinias riding upon its crest. "O, mighty Neptune," exclaimed I, with a deep groan, "take pity on us, and spare the remnants of this shipwreck; our terror has caused us already to die many deaths; if it be thy will to destroy us, do not divide us in our deaths; let one wave overwhelm us; or if we are fated to become food for the monsters of the deep let one devour us;—let us have one common death, one common tomb." I had not long uttered this prayer before the violence of the wind abated and the roughness of the waves subsided, and the surface of the sea was seen covered with floating bodies. Menelaus and his companions were thrown by the waves upon a part of the coast of Egypt which was at that time the general haunt of buccaneers. Late in the evening, Leucippe and I contrived to reach Pelusium, and upon getting to land thanked the gods for our escape; nor did we omit bewailing Clinias and Satyrus, believing them to have been drowned.

In the temple of Casian Jupiter, at Pelusium, there is the statue of a youth very like Apollo; his hand is stretched out and holds a pomegranate, which has a mystic meaning. After praying to this deity, and asking tidings of Clinias and Satyrus (for the god is believed to be prophetic) we walked about the temple; in the treasury at the rear of this edifice we saw two pictures by the artist Evanthes. The subject of one was Andromeda, of the other, Prometheus. Both were represented as bound, for which reason probably the painter had associated them together. They furnished other points of resemblance also; both had a rock for their prison house, and savage beasts for their executioners, the one being a bird of prey, the other a sea monster. The champions also who came to their rescue were both Grecians, Hercules and Perseus. The former is represented standing on the ground and aiming his arrow at the bird of Jove; the latter poised in air directs his attack against the fish. The rock is hollowed out, so as to suit the size of the maiden's body, and the rugged surface given it by the painter, plainly showed that it is intended to represent a production of nature, not the work of art; the maiden is fixed in the hollow of this rock, her lovely form giving her the appearance of a wondrously-carved statue, but the chains and the sea-monster betokening a hastily-planned tomb. Beauty and fear are mingled in her countenance, yet the pallor of her cheeks is not wholly untinged with colour, while the brightness of her eyes is tempered by a languor such as is seen in violets when they begin to fade; thus had the painter imparted to her the expression of comely fear. Her arms, extended on either side, are chained against the rock, the wrists and fingers hanging down like the clusters from the vine; her arms are of spotless white, but approaching to a livid hue, and her fingers appear bloodless. Bound in this fashion she is awaiting death. Her attire is bridal, of white, and reaching to the feet, of a texture so fine as to resemble a spider's web, the production not of the wool of sheep, but of the down of winged insects whose webs Indian women gather from the trees and weave. The monster is emerging from the sea opposite the maiden; his head alone appears above the waves, but the outline of his body is distinguishable beneath the water: the junctures of his scales, the curvature of his back, the ridge of his spines, the twisting of his tail; his immense jaws are expanded as far as his shoulders, and to the very entrance of his maw. In the intermediate space is seen Perseus descending from the sky, his body naked, with the exception of a mantle about his shoulders, winged sandals upon his feet, and a cap resembling

Pluto's helmet upon his head; in his left hand he grasps the Gorgon's head, holding it forth in the manner of a shield; the face is fearful to behold, and even on the painter's canvas seems to glare with its eyes, to bristle up its locks, to shake its serpents. His right hand is armed with a weapon between a straight sword and a scimitar; from the hilt to the middle it is a sword, it then partakes of both, remaining sharp so as to inflict a wound, and becoming curved in order to follow up and improve the stroke. Such was the "Andromeda."

Next to it, as I before remarked, was a painting of Prometheus bound to the rock. Hercules stands near him, armed with his bow and arrows. The vulture is feasting upon his side, in which it has inflicted a lacerating wound, and with its beak inserted in the opening, seems to be digging after the liver, of which the painter allows a portion to be visible. The talons of the bird are firmly planted upon the thigh of Prometheus, who shrinks with agony, contracts his side, and draws back his leg to his own hurt, for the movement brings the eagle nearer to his liver. The other leg is stretched out straight before him, and the tension of the muscles is visible to the extreme point of the toes; his whole appearance is that of acute suffering, his eyebrows are contracted, his lips drawn in, and his teeth appear; you could almost compassionate the painting, as though itself felt pain. In his misery, Hercules is come to his aid, and is preparing to transfix his tormentor; already the arrow is on the bow, which he extends with his left hand, while with his right hand he draws the string to his breast; in doing which the elbow is seen shortened from behind. The stretching of the bow, the drawing back the string, the hand touching the breast, all seemed the work of a single moment. Prometheus appears divided between hope and fear; he looks partly at his wounded side, partly at Hercules; fain would he fix his eyes upon him alone; but his agony turns them back, in part, upon himself.

After remaining two days at Pelusium to recruit ourselves after our fatigues, having fortunately some money left we engaged an Egyptian vessel, and proceeded by way of the Nile to Alexandria, with the intention of making some stay there, thinking likewise that we might find in that city some of our shipwrecked friends. Upon nearing a certain town, not far from the river, we suddenly heard a loud shout; upon which the master exclaiming, "The buccaneers are upon us!" endeavoured to put about his vessel, and to sail back, when in a moment the bark was thronged with men of formidable and savage mien. They were all tall and stout; their complexion was black,—not the jet black of the Indians, but that of a mongrel Ethiopian; they had shaven heads and very small feet, and spoke a barbarous dialect. As this was the narrowest part of the river, escape was impossible; so the master exclaiming, "We are all lost!" brought the vessel to. Four of the buccaneers came on board and carried off everything which they could lay hands on, not forgetting our stock of money; we were then taken on shore, bound and shut up in a hut, when the greater part of them rode away, leaving guards, who were to conduct us next day to the king, as their chief is styled, who, as we learnt from our fellow captives, was about two days' journey distant.

When night came on, and we were lying there bound and our guards were asleep, I found leisure to bewail Leucippe, reflecting how many calamities I had brought upon her. Deeply groaning in soul, and carefully suppressing any outward sound of grief, "Oh, ye gods and genii!" I said within myself, "if ye really exist and hear me, what heinous crimes have we committed, that in a few short days we should be plunged into such a depth of misery? And now, to crown all, ye have delivered us into the hands of Egyptian buccaneers, cutting us off from any chance of pity. Our voice and our entreaties might mollify the heart of a Grecian pirate; for words oftentimes beget compassion, and the tongue ministering to the necessities of the soul, subdues the angry feeling of the hearer; but in our present case, what language can we employ, what oaths of submission can we take? Had I tones more persuasive than the Syrens', these barbarian homicides would neither understand nor listen to me; I must then be content to supplicate with signs and gestures, and pantomimic show; it is not so much for my own misfortunes, severe as they are, which I lament, but how shall I sufficiently bewail, how sufficiently weep for thine, Leucippe, thou who hast shown thyself so faithful in all the straits of love, so tender towards thy unhappy lover! Behold, the splendid preparation for thy marriage; a prison for thy bridal chamber, earth for thy couch, the noose and the rope for thy necklaces and bracelets, a pirate for thy bridesman, a dirge for thy nuptial hymn. O Sea! I have thanked thee without reason; rather should I upbraid thee for thy mercy; greater in reality has been thy kindness to those whom thou hast drowned; our preservation deserves rather to be called destruction, for thou hast grudged us death except by the hands of buccaneers." In this manner did I inwardly lament, but no tears came to my relief; this is indeed peculiar to the eyes in all great misfortunes; in the season of any ordinary grief, they flow readily enough, and then they not only serve as intercessors between the sufferer and the cause of his sufferings, but they also diminish the inward swelling of the heart; but in the time of excessive sorrow, tears take to flight and are traitors to the eyes; sorrow encounters them as they are springing from their fountain, arrests their progress and compels them to retrace their way; accordingly, turned from the direction of the eyes they flow back upon the soul and exasperate its inward wounds.

Turning to Leucippe, who had not spoken a word, I said, "Why are you silent, dearest? Why do you not speak to me?" "Because," she replied, "though my soul still lives, my voice is already dead." The dawn imperceptibly overtook us while we were engaged in conversation, when a horseman suddenly rode up with a profusion of long matted hair; his horse was as shaggy as himself and bare-backed, without housings of any kind, as is customary with the horses of these buccaneers. He came it appeared from their captain, with orders to bring away any maiden whom he might find to be an expiatory offering on behalf of the pirates, to their god. The guards immediately seized Leucippe, who clung to me with shrieks, but while some of them struck me, others tore her away, placed her on horseback and rode away, leaving us who were still bound to follow at greater leisure. We had scarcely proceeded two furlongs from the village when we heard a loud shouting mingled with the sounds of a trumpet, and presently a body of heavy armed soldiers appeared in view, upon which the pirates, placing us in the centre, stood their ground and prepared for resistance. The soldiers were about fifty in number, some bearing long shields reaching to the feet, others having only bucklers. The buccaneers, who were far superior in numbers, began to pelt the military with clods of earth: now, an Egyptian clod can do more execution than any other, for being of stony earth, it is at the same time heavy, rough, and jagged, can raise a swelling and inflict a wound. The soldiers relying upon the protection of their shields cared little for these missiles, and waiting till the buccaneers were tired with their exertions, they suddenly opened their ranks, when the light-armed darted out, each armed with a javelin and a sword, and so skilful was the aim that no one missed his mark; the heavy-armed proceeded to support them and a stubborn fight took place, in which abundance of blows and wounds were exchanged on either side. Military discipline made up for deficiency of numbers, the pirates began to give ground, which, when we observed, I and the other prisoners bursting through their ranks went over to the enemy; ignorant of our real condition the soldiers were about to kill us, when perceiving us to be naked and bound with cords, they received us into their ranks and sent us for safety to the rear; meanwhile a body of cavalry came up and extending their flanks they surrounded the buccaneers, got them into a narrow space and cut them down; the greater part were soon dispatched, some though severely wounded still resisted, the rest were taken prisoners. It was now about evening; the commander of the forces, Charmides by name, interrogated us severally, asking who we were, and how we had been captured. The others told their stories and I related my own adventures; after hearing every particular he desired us to follow him, promising to supply us with arms; it being his intention, as soon as the rest of his troops came up, to attack the chief haunt of the pirates, where it was said there were ten thousand men. Being a good rider I requested the favour of a horse, and no sooner was my wish complied with, than mounting I went through the different evolutions of a cavalry soldier, to the great delight of the commander. He insisted on having me as a guest at his own table, and after hearing my history at supper time, expressed his commiseration of my misfortunes.

The listening to others' grief often times begets sympathy in the hearers, and this sympathy leads to friendship, the soul affected by the relation of woe, passing from feelings of pity to sensations of a tenderer kind. Charmides, at any rate, was so much moved, that he could not refrain from tears; more than this he could not do, as Leucippe was in the power of the pirates. I may also mention that he kindly gave me an Egyptian as my servant. The next day he prepared to advance against the buccaneers, who were seen in great force on the other side of a trench which it was his object to fill up. They had constructed a rude altar of earth, and near it lay a coffin; two men were seen conducting the maiden, whose hands were bound behind her back.

I could not distinguish who they were, because their armour concealed them, but I easily recognized Leucippe. After pouring a libation upon her head, they led her round the altar, an Egyptian priest all the while chanting a hymn as was evident from the motion of his lips and the muscles of his face; when this was ended, all at a signal being given retired to a considerable distance, when one of the young men who had conducted the maiden placed her upon the ground, bound her to four wooden pegs——just as image makers represent Marsyas bound to the tree—and then drawing a sword plunged it into her heart, and drawing the weapon downwards laid open all her belly so that the intestines immediately protruded; then they removed and laid them upon the altar, and when roasted they were cut into portions and partaken of by the pirates. The soldiers and their commander upon witnessing these proceedings cried out and averted their faces in disgust; strange to say, I continued to gaze in stupid astonishment, as if thunderstruck by the surpassing horror of the spectacle. There may really have been some truth in the legend of Niobe, and from being affected by the loss of her children, in the same way in which I was now, her motionless appearance may have given her the appearance of being turned to stone. When the horrible business was, as I supposed ended, the young men placed the body in the coffin, covering it with a lid, and after throwing down the altar, hurried back to their companions, not once looking behind them, for such had been the injunction of the priest.

By evening the trench was filled up and the soldiers after crossing it, encamped for the night and prepared their supper. Charmides seeing my distress, did all in his power to console me, but to no purpose; for about the first watch of the night, when all were asleep, I took my sword, proceeded to the spot and prepared to stab myself upon the coffin.— "Wretched Leucippe," I exclaimed, "thou most ill-fated of human kind, I lament not so much thy death, nor thy dying in a foreign land, nor that it has been a death of violence; but that such insults have been heaped upon thy misfortunes—that thou hast been made a victim to purify the most polluted of their kind—that thou hast been ripped up while yet alive, and able to gaze upon the horrid process—that thou hast had an accursed altar and coffin for thy joint grave, the former for thy bowels, the latter for thy body. Had the fire consumed thy entrails, there would be less cause to grieve; but now, most horrible, they have been made to furnish forth food to a pirate band! O accursed altar-torch, O unheard of banquet! and yet the gods looked quietly down upon such proceedings, and yet the fire was not extinguished, but polluted as it was sent up its odour with acceptance to the deities! Leucippe, thou shalt now receive from me the offering which befits thee." After uttering these words, I raised the sword and was on the point of stabbing myself, when by the light of the moon I perceived two men hastily running towards me; supposing them to be buccaneers, I paused in the expectation of being put to death by them; they soon reached the spot where I was standing and both called aloud to me, and who should they prove to be, but Satyrus and Menelaus. So profound was my grief at what had taken place, that though I saw before me two of my friends unexpectedly alive and well, I neither embraced them nor felt any emotion of joy.

Seizing my hand they endeavoured to wrest the sword from me. "In the name of the gods," said I, "grudge me not a welcome death, or rather, I should say, a medicine for all my ills. Do what you please; I will no longer remain in life, now that Leucippe is gone. You may indeed deprive me of this weapon, but there will remain a sword of grief within which slowly kills and drinks my blood; do you wish that I should die by this slow and lingering death?" Upon this, interrupting me, Menelaus said, "If this be your only reason for dying, you may put up your sword; Leucippe shall soon come to life again." I looked steadfastly at him, and exclaimed, "Can you insult me in the midst of such calamities?—have some regard for hospitable Jove." Without farther delay he tapped upon the coffin several times, calling out, "Leucippe, since Clitopho is incredulous, do you bear witness to the truth of what I say;" and almost immediately a faint voice was heard proceeding from the interior. A sudden trembling seized me, and I gazed upon Menelaus, half believing him to be a sorcerer; he proceeded to remove the lid, when Leucippe slowly rose and came forth, presenting the most fearful spectacle which can be imagined; the lower part of her person was entirely laid open and all her bowels had been removed; we rushed into each other's embrace and both fell to the ground. When I had recovered myself a little, I said to Menelaus, "Will you not explain the meaning of all this? Is not this Leucippe whose face I behold, whose form I press, and whose voice I hear? What was it which I witnessed yesterday? Either it was an idle dream, or what I now see is an unreality; and yet this kiss is warm, loving, and sweet, as Leucippe's was wont to be."—"Her bowels shall soon be restored," was his reply; "the wound on her breast shall be healed, and you shall behold her sound as ever, but be so good as to cover your eyes, for I must call Hecate to lend us her assistance."

Believing him in earnest I followed his directions, and he began to practise his juggling tricks and to mutter certain sounds, at the same time removing the contrivances from Leucippe's body and restoring her to her usual appearance. "Uncover your face," he at length exclaimed. Slowly and with great trepidation—for I really believed that Hecate was there—I removed my hands from my eyes, and beheld Leucippe's own sweet self, unharmed in any way: more astonished than ever, "My dear Menelaus," said I, "if you are the minister of any god, tell me where we are, and what all these things mean."—"Do not frighten him any more," interrupted Leucippe, "but at once tell him how you contrived to outwit the buccaneers."—"You may remember my telling you on board ship," said Menelaus, "that I am by birth an Egyptian; my property lies chiefly about this village, and I am consequently well acquainted with the principal persons in it; when I and Satyrus after being shipwrecked were thrown on shore we were conducted into the presence of the pirate chief; some of his people soon recognized me, upon which my chains were taken off, and after assuring me of safety I was strongly urged to join their company as being in some degree already known to them. Upon this I required that Satyrus should be delivered up to me, declaring him to be a slave of mine: 'Your wish shall be complied with,' they replied, 'provided you first give some proof of courage in our cause.' Fortunately they had just then been commanded by an oracle to offer up a virgin as an expiation for their robber band, and after tasting the victim's entrails they were to place the body in a coffin and to retire from the scene of sacrifice. The object of this was to strike terror into the minds of the hostile force; but," continued he, addressing Satyrus, "the rest of the story belongs more properly to you."

"Upon learning that Leucippe was taken captive," said Satyrus, taking up the narrative, "I felt sincere regret on her behalf, and urged Menelaus by all means to save her; some good genius came to our assistance; the day before the sacrifice we were sitting by the sea-shore, overcome with grief and considering what steps were to be taken. Some of the buccaneers espying a vessel which had got out of her course from ignorance of the coast, hurried down to attack her; the crew endeavoured to put out to sea, but being too late they prepared for resistance.

"There happened to be among them a stage-player or reciter of Homeric poetry. Arming himself and the rest after the manner of the heroes of the Iliad, they offered a brave resistance, but being at last overpowered by a number of the pirate boats, their vessel was sunk and themselves were slaughtered. It chanced that after this a chest floated on shore unperceived by the buccaneers; Menelaus getting it into a retired spot opened it, supposing it might contain something valuable; among the contents were a cloak and a sword with a hilt five palms in length, the blade of which was not so long: while Menelaus was carelessly handling it, the blade flew out and became equal to the hilt in length, and a different movement reduced it, to its former dimensions; the ill-fated owner had no doubt been accustomed to use it upon the stage for the infliction of mimic wounds. I immediately said to Menelaus, 'if only you will now give proof of your courage, the deity will second us, and we shall be able to preserve the maiden without being discovered by the buccaneers. We will get a sheepskin, one of the softest and most flexible which can be procured, this we will sew into the shape of a bag, corresponding in size with the human stomach, and after filling it with entrails and blood, we will secure the opening; having done this, we will fasten it upon the maiden's body, and by throwing over her a robe bound by a girdle and other fastenings we can easily conceal the artifice. The nature of the oracle given to the pirates and the construction of the sword, are both strongly in our favour: the oracle commands that the maiden when adorned for sacrifice is to be ripped open through her dress; and as for the sword, you see how artfully it is contrived; if you press it against the human body, the blade flies into the hilt as into a scabbard, while all the time it will appear to the beholders to have been run into the body; on the present occasion just enough of the blade will remain out to cut open the false stomach as soon as the hilt reaches the sheepskin, and when withdrawn from the wound, the portion of the sword contained within the hilt will immediately fly out, so that it will appear to the spectator that the whole of the weapon was really plunged into the maiden. The pirates will not discover the deceit, for as I before said, the skin will be concealed by the dress put over it, and the entrails will immediately protrude from the gash which it has made; these we shall place upon the altar, and as no one is to approach the body, we shall be able to place it in the coffin. You remember the pirate-captain telling you that you were expected to display some proof of courage; now is the time to go to him and to make the offer.'

"I followed up my words by many entreaties, invoking Jove the hospitable, and reminding Menelaus of our having eaten at the same board and suffered the same perils of shipwreck. The worthy and true hearted man replied, 'The undertaking is arduous, but one ought to be prepared to die in the sake of a friend, and death in such a cause is sweet.' I then expressed my belief that Clitopho was still alive, for the maiden had mentioned to me his being left behind, among the other prisoners, in addition to which the buccaneers who had fled, brought word to their captain, that all the captives had contrived to escape into the enemy's ranks during the engagement. 'You will therefore,' I added, 'be doing him a very great kindness and will also be the means of delivering this unhappy maiden out of her misfortunes.' I succeeded in persuading him, and Fortune favoured us in our undertaking. While I was busied in preparing what was needed for our contrivance, Menelaus proceeded to the buccaneers to make the proposal already mentioned. The chief, by a lucky chance, anticipated him, and said, 'We have a law, that new comers amongst us, should first begin the sacrifice, especially when a human victim is to be offered; be ready therefore against to-morrow; your slave also must take part in the solemnity.'—'We will endeavour,' replied Menelaus, 'to show ourselves not inferior to any among yourselves.'—'Remember,' added the pirate-chief, 'that it will be for you to dress and arrange the maiden in the best manner for consummating the sacrifice.' Afterwards, when alone, we took the opportunity of fitting out Leucippe in the manner before related, bidding her have no fear, and carefully instructing her what to do, enjoining her to remain quiet in the coffin, if necessary, the whole day, but when an opportunity offered to seek safety by flying to the encampment; having given her these directions we led her to the altar: what afterwards occurred you already know."

While listening to this narrative, I was overwhelmed by a variety of feelings, and did not know how sufficiently to express my deep gratitude to Menelaus; I however adopted the most common method, and throwing myself at his feet, I embraced his knees and worshipped him as a god, my heart thrilling with delight. Being now easy concerning Leucippe, "What," I inquired, "has become of Clinias?" "The last time I saw him," replied Menelaus, "was when he was clinging to the yard after the shipwreck; what afterwards became of him I cannot tell."

Upon hearing this, I could not repress a cry of grief in the midst of my joy; no doubt some malignant genius envied me the possession of pure and unalloyed happiness; for this cause doubtless, he whom next to Leucippe I most valued, was especially selected as a victim by the sea, that not only his soul might perish, but that he might lose the rights of sepulture. Oh, ruthless ocean, thus to curtail the full measure of thy mercy towards us!

There being nothing to detain us longer, we all repaired to the encampment, and passed the rest of the night in my tent; nor was it long before the adventure became known. At daybreak, conducting Menelaus to the commander, I related every particular; Charmides was highly pleased, and expressed himself in the most friendly terms towards him. He next inquired what the strength of the enemy amounted to. Menelaus replied, "That the whole place was full of desperate men, and that the buccaneers numbered perhaps ten thousand men."

"Our five thousand," said Charmides, "will be a match for twenty thousand such as they are: besides which two thousand men will shortly arrive from the troops who garrison the Delta and Heliopolis." While he was still speaking, a boy came in and said that an express had come from the camp in the Delta, to announce that the expected reinforcement would not arrive for five days; the incursions of the buccaneers in that quarter had been repressed indeed, but when the troops were on the point of marching, the sacred bird, bearing the sepulchre of his father, had appeared among them, and on this account the march must be delayed during the period mentioned.

"And pray," inquired I, "what bird is this which is treated with such respect? What sepulchre is it which he carries with him?"—"He is called the Phœnix," was the reply; "and is a native of Ethiopia; he is about the size of the peacock, but superior to him in beauty; his plumage is bedropt with gold and purple, and he boasts of being descended from the sun, a claim which is borne out by the appearance of his head, which is crowned by a splendid circle, the very image of that orb. The hues are mingled rose and azure, and the disposition of the feathers represent the rays. He belongs to the Ethiopians during his life, but the Egyptians possess him after he is dead. He is very long lived, and upon his decease; his son bears him to the Nile, having first prepared his sepulchre in the following manner. Taking a mass of the most fragrant myrrh, sufficient for the purpose, he excavates the centre with his beak, and the hollow becomes a receptacle for the dead; then closing up the aperture with earth, he soars aloft and carries this fruit of his pious labour to the Nile. A flight of other birds attends him, as a guard of honour, and he resembles a monarch making a progress. He never deviates from the place of his destination, the city of the sun, which is the resting-place of the departed bird; upon arriving there he stations himself upon an elevated spot, and awaits the arrival of the minister of religion. Presently an Egyptian priest comes forth from the sanctuary, bearing a book containing a picture of the bird, in order that he may judge whether it be genuine. The phœnix, aware of this, opens the receptacle, and exhibiting the body, makes intercession for its interment; after which it is received by the sons of the priest and buried; thus, as I have already observed, this bird is an Ethiopian during his lifetime, but makes his grave with the Egyptians."

Book IV

U pon hearing of the preparations made by the buccaneers, and of the march of the reinforcements being postponed, Charmides resolved upon returning to his former quarters, and there to await their arrival. A lodging was assigned by him to Leucippe and me at a little distance. No sooner had I entered it, than taking her in my arms, I endeavoured to accomplish my wishes; she would not consent however, upon which I said to her: "Do you not observe how many strange and unforeseen accidents befall us; first we are shipwrecked, then we come into the hands of pirates, and next you are exposed to be sacrificed, and to undergo a cruel death. Fortune has just now lulled the storm, let us, therefore, take advantage of the opportunity, before any yet severer calamity overtakes us."

"It is not lawful for me to consent now," was her reply; "for while I was bewailing myself at the prospect of being sacrificed, the goddess Diana appeared to me in a dream and said: 'Weep not, maiden, thou shalt not die; I will protect thee, and thou must remain a virgin until I conduct thee to thine husband, who shall be Clitopho, and no one else.'"

Upon hearing this circumstance, I was very much annoyed at the delay, but yet rejoiced at the prospect of future happiness opened to me; and her mention of the dream reminded me of something similar which had happened to myself. I thought that during the preceding night I saw the temple of Venus, and could discern the statue of the goddess within; upon approaching it with the design of offering up my prayers, the doors were suddenly closed, and while standing there in a state of disappointment, a female strongly resembling the statue of the goddess appeared to me and said: "It is not permitted thee to enter the temple now; but if thou wilt wait for a short period, I will not only open to thee its doors, but will constitute thee my priest." I related this dream to Leucippe, and although my attempts upon her chastity were not repeated, I could not get over my feelings of vexation.

An occurrence which just then took place gave Charmides an opportunity of seeing Leucippe and conceiving a passion for her. Some person had captured a very curious river animal, called by the Egyptians the Nile-horse, and in truth he resembles that animal in his belly and legs, except that he has cloven hoofs; his size is equal to that of the largest ox; he has a short tail, which as well as his body, is devoid of hair; his head is large and round, with cheeks like those of a horse; his nostrils are widely expanded and breathe out sparks, as it were, of fiery vapours; he has an immense under-jaw, which opens to nearly the length of his head, and it is garnished with canine teeth like those of a horse in shape and position, but three times as large. We were invited to see this creature, and looked at it with great interest; but the eyes of the commander were rivetted upon Leucippe, of whom he immediately became enamoured.

In order to detain us there the longer, and by this means to feast his own eyes, he entered upon a lengthy description of the animal, its nature and habits, and the manner in which it is captured; that it is so voracious as to eat up a whole field of corn, and is taken by employing the following stratagem. Having found out his usual haunt, the hunters dig a deep pit, which they cover with reeds and earth, underneath is placed a wooden chest with open doors which reach to the top of the pit. The animal in passing over the spot at once falls into the chest as into a cave, when the hunters, who have been on the watch, immediately close the doors, and in this manner secure their prey. It would be in vain to attempt capturing him by force; for not only is he very powerful, but has a hide so hard and thick as to render him proof against any wounds; he may be called the Egyptian elephant, and in strength comes next to the elephant of India.

"Have you ever seen an elephant?" inquired Menelaus. "I have," replied Charmides, "and have conversed with persons well acquainted with the peculiarity attending its birth."

I here remarked that the animal was known to me only having seen a picture of it. "Well, then," continued he, "I will give you an account of it; for we have abundance of leisure. The time of gestation with the female is ten years, so that when she brings forth her calf he is already old. To this cause we may, in my opinion, attribute his great bulk, his unrivalled strength, and his longevity; for he is said to live longer than Hesiod's crow. His jaw may be said to resemble the head of an ox, for it appears to have two horns; these, however, are the curved tusks of the animal, between them projects his trunk, resembling a trumpet in appearance and size, which is very convenient for taking up his accustomed food or any other edible; anything of this description he seizes with it, and bending it inwards, conveys it to his mouth; but if unsuited for his palate, he turns round his trunk, and extending it upwards delivers the article to the Ethiopian master, who sits upon him as a rider does on a horse, and whom he caresses and also fears, obeying his voice, and submitting to be beaten with an iron axe. I remember once seeing a strange sight, a Greek inserted his head into the mouth of the animal, which with expanded jaws continued to breathe upon him. As you may imagine, I was not a little struck with the boldness of the man and the good-nature of the elephant. The man told me that he had given the beast a fee for breathing upon him, that his breath was almost equal to Indian spices, and was a sovereign specific against the head-ache. It appears that the elephant is aware of his medical skill, and will not open his mouth for nothing, but like a self-conceited physician, asks for his fee beforehand; upon receiving it he becomes all complaisance, expands his jaws, and keeps his mouth open as long as the patient pleases, knowing that he has received a consideration for his breath."

"How comes so ill-favoured an animal to have so fragrant a breath?" I asked. "From the nature of the food upon which he feeds," said Charmides. "The country of the Indians is near the sun; they first behold the rising of that deity, they feel his hottest rays, and from his influence their skin acquires its hue. Now there is in Greece a dark-coloured flower, which among the Indians is not a flower but a leaf, like those which are seen on any tree; in that land it conceals its fragrance, and is therefore in little estimation; either it does not care for celebrity among its countrymen, or else it grudges them its sweetness; but if only it leave that country and be transplanted, it opens its secret treasure-house, instead of a leaf becomes a flower, and clothes itself with perfume. The Indians call this the black rose, and it is as common a food for the elephant as among us grass is for oxen; and from feeding upon it, almost from its birth, the animal exhales the fragrance of his food, and his breath becomes a fount of sweets."

When Charmides had ended his dissertation and we were departed, he not long after—for whoever burns with the fire of love cannot endure delay—sent for Menelaus, and taking his hand, thus addressed him:—"Your conduct to Clitopho shows you to be a sincere friend, nor shall you have to complain of want of friendship upon my part. I have a favour to request which it is easy for you to grant, and by granting it you will preserve my life. Know that I am desperately smitten with Leucippe; you must heal the wound; she is in your debt for having saved her. Now I will give you fifty gold pieces for the good service which I require, and she herself shall receive as many as she pleases."

"Keep your gold," replied Menelaus, "for those who make a traffic of their favours; you have already received me into your friendship, and it shall be my endeavour to promote your wishes."

Immediately afterwards he came to me and related the whole matter. After deliberating what course to adopt, dissimulation appeared most feasible, since it would have been dangerous to give him an absolute refusal, for fear of his employing violence, and it was wholly out of our power to escape, surrounded as we were by the buccaneers in one direction, and by his troops on the other.

Returning to Charmides after a short interval, Menelaus said:— "Your object is accomplished. At first the maiden gave a downright refusal, but at length, upon my redoubling my entreaties and reminding her of her debt of gratitude towards me, she consented; stipulating, however, for a few days' delay until we can reach Alexandria; for this place being a mere village, everything becomes known, and there are many eyes upon us."

"You fix a long postponement to your favour," said Charmides. "Who can think of deferring his wishes in time of war? With an engagement before him, and so many ways of death, how can the soldier tell whether his life will be spared? If you will prevail on Fortune to guarantee my safety, I will wait. Consider that I am about to fight these buccaneers, and all the while a war of a different kind is raging in my soul; a warrior armed with bow and arrow, is committing havoc there; I feel myself vanquished; I am full of wounds; prithee send for the leech with speed, for the danger presses. I shall have to carry fire and sword among the enemy, but love has already kindled his torch to my destruction; extinguish this flame, I beseech, good Menelaus; it will be a fair omen to join in love before we join in battle; let Venus, therefore, herald me on my way to Mars."

"But you do not consider," rejoined Menelaus, "how difficult it is to avoid discovery from her intended husband, who is so enamoured of her."—"Oh! as for Clitopho, we can easily get him out of the way," said Charmides.

Seeing him so firmly bent upon his purpose, Menelaus began to have fears for my safety, and suddenly he thought himself of a fresh excuse. "If you must know her real motive for this delay, it is that her monthly sickness is upon her, consequently she must abstain from sexual intercourse."—"In that case," said the other, "I will wait three or four days, which will be quite sufficient; but in the meanwhile she can, at any rate, come and talk to me. I can hear her voice, press her hand, and touch her person, and kiss her lips. Her indisposition need be no impediment to this."

When Menelaus told this to me, I exclaimed, that I would sooner die than have Leucippe bestow her lips upon another. "A kiss," I said, "is the best part of love; the moment of actual enjoyment is soon over, and brings with it satiety, and is indeed worth nothing if we take away the kissing. A kiss need have no limit to its duration; it never cloys, it is always new. Three things, excellent in their nature, proceed from the mouth, the breath, the voice, and last of all, the kiss, of which the lips are the instruments, but the seat of pleasure is in the soul. Believe me, Menelaus, for my troubles compel me to reveal the secret, these are the only favours which I have received from Leucippe; she is a woman only as having been kissed by me; in all other respects she is still a virgin. I will not put up with the loss of them; I will not have my kisses adulterously dallied with."

"If such be the case," said Menelaus, "we must speedily resolve upon some plan; one who is in love (like Charmides) as long as he has a hope of success will wait and feed on expectation, but if driven to despair, his love changes into hate and urges him to take vengeance upon the obstacle to his desires; and supposing he has the power to do this with impunity, the very fact of being free from fear deepens his resentment and urges him on to his revenge." In the midst of our deliberation some one hastily entered, and informed us that Leucippe while walking about had suddenly fallen down, and lay there wildly rolling her eyes. We hurried to her, and finding her still lying on the ground, we asked what ailed her? No sooner did she see me, than starting up and glaring fiercely from her blood-shot eyes, she struck me with violence upon the face, and when Menelaus endeavoured to support her, she proceeded to kick his shins. Perceiving that she was labouring under frenzy, we seized her by main force and endeavoured to overpower her, she on her part resisted, and in her struggles was at no pains to hide what women generally wish to keep concealed. So great was the disturbance that at length the commander himself came in, and witnessed what was going on. At first he was suspicious of some fraud contrived against himself, and looked sternly upon Menelaus; but seeing the truth, he became moved by feelings of compassion.

Meanwhile cords were brought and the unhappy maiden was bound; upon seeing her hands confined in this manner, I besought Menelaus (all but a few having left the tent) to set her arms at liberty; "her tender arms," I said, "cannot endure this harsh treatment; leave me with her alone; my arms shall be her fetters, and she may exhaust her frenzy upon, me: why, indeed, should I wish to live, since Leucippe no longer knows me? How can I behold her lying thus bound, and though having the power, shew no desire to release her? Has Fortune delivered us from the hands of buccaneers only that she may fall a prey to madness? Unhappy that we are, when will our condition change? We escape dangers at home only to be overtaken by the shipwreck; saved from the fury of the sea and freed from pirates, we were reserved for the present visitation—madness! Even shouldst thou recover thy senses, dearest, I fear lest the evil genius may have something worse in store! Who can be pronounced more unhappy than ourselves, who have cause to dread even what bears the appearance of good fortune! Let Fortune, however, again make us her sport, provided only I can see thee restored to health and sense!" Menelaus and those present did all they could to comfort me, saying that such maladies were not lasting, and were very common in the hot season of youth; at such a time the young blood, heated by the vigour of the body, runs boiling through the veins, and overflowing the brain drowns the powers of reason; the proper course, therefore, would be to have medical advice.

Menelaus went to the commander without delay, and requested that the physician belonging to the troops might be called in. Charmides readily complied, for a lover delights in granting favours. After visiting her, he said, "we must make her sleep in order to subdue the paroxysm of her disease; for sleep is the medicine of every sickness, and afterwards we will have recourse to other means." Before leaving her, he gave us a portion of some drug, about the size of a pea, which was to be dissolved in oil and rubbed upon the top of her head, saying that he would shortly bring a pill to act upon her bowels. We followed his directions, and after her head had been rubbed for a short time, she fell asleep, and slept till morning. I sat by her bed side all night in tears, and when I saw the cords which still confined her hands, I could not help exclaiming, "Dearest Leucippe, bondage is still thy portion; not even in sleep is liberty allowed thee! What images, I wonder, are now passing before thy mind? Does sense attend upon thy sleep? or do thy dreams also partake of frenzy?" Upon waking she uttered some incoherent words. Soon after the physician came and administered the other medicine.

Just at this time pressing orders arrived from the Viceroy of Egypt urging the commander to lead his men against the enemy. The troops were immediately mustered with their officers, and appeared on the ground in marching order, when, after giving them the watchword, he dismissed them to their quarters for the night, and next morning led them out to battle.

I will now describe the nature of the district against which they marched. The Nile flows in an unbroken stream from Egyptian Thebes as far as Memphis, when it throws out a small branch. Where the wide part of the river terminates, stands the village Cercasorum; there the country becomes intersected by three streams; two flowing respectively to the right and left; the other continuing its onward course traverses the district called the Delta; none of these streams flow uninterruptedly to the sea, but upon reaching different cities separate into various branches, all of them larger than any Grecian rivers; its waters nevertheless are not enfeebled and rendered useless by the many divisions in their course; they bear vessels upon their surface; they are used for drinking, and contribute to fertilize the land. The mighty Nile is all in all to the Egyptians, both land and river, and sea and lake, and a singular spectacle it is to see in juxtaposition the ship and the mattock, the oar and the plough, the rudder and the hook, sailors' cabins and labourers' huts, a resort for fishes and a resting-place for oxen; where but lately a ship sailed, is seen a cultivated plain, and anon the cultivated plain becomes a watery space; for the Nile periodically comes and goes, and the Egyptians count the days and anxiously await the inundation, while the river on his part keeps to his appointed time, regulates the rising of his waters, and never exposes himself to the imputation of unpunctuality. Then comes the rivalry between the land and water; each exerts its power against the other; the water strives to flood the land, and the land does its endeavour to absorb the fertilizing water; in the end, conquest can be assigned to neither, but both may claim the victory, for each is co-extensive with the other. In the pasturage which is the resort of the buccaneers, a quantity of water is at all times found, for even when the Nile retires, the lakes formed by its inundation continue filled with watery mud; over these the inhabitants can either wade on foot or pass in boats, each of which will contain one person; any other kind would be imbedded in the mud, but those which they employ are so light as to require very little water, and should none be found they take them on their backs, and proceed on foot until they arrive at more. These lakes, which I have mentioned, are dotted over with islets, some of them uninhabited, but abounding in papyrus reeds, between the intervals of which there is only room for a man to stand, while the space above is overarched by the summits of the leaves; it is in these places that the buccaneers assemble, and secretly concert their plans, masked by these reeds as by a fort. Some of the islets have huts upon them, presenting the appearance of a rudely constructed town, which serve as the dwellings of the pirates. One of them, more remarkable than the other for its extent and for the number of its huts, was called Nicochis, and here it was that the main body of the freebooters was collected; confiding in their numbers, and in the strength of their position, the place being entirely insulated by lagoons, except for a narrow causeway the eighth of a mile long and seventy feet wide. As soon as they were aware of the commander's approach, they had recourse to the following stratagem:—mustering all the old men, they equipped them as suppliants, with palm branches, commanding the most able-bodied among the youth to follow, armed with swords and shields. The old men were to hold aloft their suppliant branches, the foliage of which would serve to conceal those in the rear, who, by way of farther precaution, were directed to stoop and trail their spears along the ground.

In case the commander yielded to the old men's supplications, the others were to make no hostile movements; if, on the contrary, he should reject their entreaties, they were to invite him to their city, with the offer of there surrendering themselves up to death; if he agreed to follow them, upon arriving at the middle of the narrow causeway, the old men, at a preconcerted signal, were to throw away their branches and make their escape, while the others were to make an assault with might and main. They proceeded to execute these directions, and upon approaching the commander, entreated him to reverence their old age and suppliant branches, and to take pity upon their town; they offered him a present of a hundred talents of silver for himself, together with an hundred hostages, to be forwarded by him to the seat of government.

They were quite sincere in making these proposals, and would have fulfilled them faithfully had he consented; upon his refusal, "We must then," said they, "submit to our destiny; at least grant us this one favour: do not put us to death at a distance from our town, conduct us to our 'fatherland,' to our hearths and homes, and there let us find our grave. We ourselves are ready to lead the way!" Upon hearing these words,

Charmides laid aside his dispositions for battle, and ordered his forces to follow leisurely. The buccaneers had meanwhile posted some scouts at a distance, who were to watch the movements of the enemy, and who, when they had reached the causeway, were to let out the waters upon them. The canals which issue from the branches of the Nile have high banks, to hinder the river from flooding the land before the time, and when the fields require watering, a portion of the bank is cut through. Now there was a long and wide canal behind the town which we are speaking of; those who were stationed for the purpose cut through the banks as soon as they saw the enemy approaching, and in a moment the old men fled, the others charged with their spears, on rolled the waters rising higher and higher, the causeway was flooded, and all around became a sea.

The buccaneers at the first onset speared the foremost of the enemy, together with their commander, who were taken by surprise, and therefore quite unprepared, and it is difficult to describe the various ways in which the others perished. Some fell before they could even handle their weapons; some before they could offer any resistance; for to see their assailants and to receive their own death-wound was simultaneous; others were slain before they could see the hand which slew them; some overcome by terror, remained motionless awaiting death; others upon attempting to move were taken off their legs by the force of the stream, while others again, who had betaken themselves to flight, were carried along and drowned in the deep part of the lagoons, where the water was above their heads; those even who were upon land had water up to their middles, which, by turning aside their shields, exposed their bodies to the enemy. The difficulty of knowing what was land and what was not, retarded many, and was the cause of their being taken prisoners; while others supposing themselves still on land came into deep water and were drowned; here were to be seen mishaps and wrecks of an unwonted kind,—a land engagement on the water, and a wreck upon the land.

The buccaneers were greatly elated by their success, and attributed their victory not to fraud but to their own valour; for among the Egyptians their fear degenerates into abject cowardice, and their courage mounts to rashness; in this respect they are always in extremes, and are wholly subject either to the excess or the defect. Ten days had now passed and Leucippe was no better; upon one occasion while asleep she cried out in a frenzied manner, "Gorgias, it is thou who hast driven me mad!" I told Menelaus of this in the morning, and began to consider whether there was any one in the village of that name. We were just going out, when a young man met and accosted me, saying, "I am come to save you and your wife." Perfectly astounded, and thinking that his coming was providential, "Are you Gorgias?" I inquired.—"No," replied he, "my name is Chæreas; Gorgias is the cause of all the mischief." I felt a thrill run through me, as I asked, "What mischief do you mean? Who is Gorgias? Some deity betrayed his name to me last night; be you an interpreter of the announcement."

"Gorgias," he resumed, "was an Egyptian soldier; he is now no more, having been slain by the buccaneers. He conceived a passion for your wife, and being well acquainted with the nature of drugs, he compounded a love philtre which he persuaded your Egyptian servant to mix with Leucippe's drink; he neglected to dilute the potion, so that instead of producing love it brought on madness. I was informed of all this yesterday by Gorgias' servant, who accompanied his master against the buccaneers, and who seems to have been specially preserved by Fortune for your sake. He asks four pieces of gold for effecting your wife's recovery, having, as he says, a drug which will counteract the effects of that which has been administered." "All blessings attend you for this good service!" I exclaimed; "pray bring the man here of whom you speak."

No sooner was he departed on this errand, than going in to the Egyptian, I struck him repeatedly about the head with my clenched fist, saying at every blow, "What was it which you gave Leucippe? What is it which has caused her madness?" The fellow in his fright confessed everything, confirming what Chæreas had already said; upon which we thrust him into prison, and there kept him. By this time Chæreas had returned, bringing the man with him. "Here are your four gold pieces as the reward for your seasonable information; but before you proceed to do anything, hear my opinion. As this lady's illness has been caused by swallowing a drug, I cannot but think it dangerous to administer more physic while the stomach is already under the influence of medicine; tell me, therefore, what are the ingredients in your proposed remedy, and compound it in my presence; upon these conditions I will give you four more gold pieces." "Your apprehensions are reasonable," he replied; "but the ingredients in my medicine are all common and fit for human food, and I will myself swallow the same quantity which I give the lady." After specifying the various ingredients, he sent some one out to procure them; and as soon as they were brought, he pounded them together in our presence, made two draughts of them, saying, "one of them I will drink off, the other is for the lady; it will make her sleep all night, and in the morning she will awake quite recovered." He then swallowed the draught, and ordered the other to be taken at night. "I must now go and lie down," he said, "under the influence of the medicine." With these words he left us, having received the stipulated sum, and with the assurance of the additional reward being paid him, if Leucippe should recover. When the hour arrived for administering the draught, I poured it out, and thus addressed it:

"Offspring of the Earth, gift of Æsculapius, may the promises made of thee be verified; shew thyself propitious and preserve my beloved; subdue the power of that ruthless potion." Thus having entered into a kind of compact with the medicine, I kissed the cup and give it to Leucippe. She soon fell into a profound sleep, and while sitting beside her I said to her, as if she could still hear me, "Wilt thou really recover thy senses? Wilt thou know me again? Shall I hear that dear voice of thine? Give some token in thy sleep, as yesternight thou didst concerning Gorgias; happier are thy sleeping than thy waking hours; frenzy is thy portion when awake, but thou art inspired by Wisdom when asleep."

At length my words and thoughts were interrupted by the anxiously-expected break of day, and I heard Leucippe's voice calling me by name. Instantly I hurried to her side, and inquired how she felt; she appeared to have no knowledge of what had passed, and seeing that her hands were bound, expressed surprise, and inquired who had tied them. Finding her restored to her right mind, I undid the knots in great agitation, through excess of joy, and then related to her all particulars. She blushed upon learning what had passed, and almost believed herself to be still committing the same extravagance; but my assurances gradually soothed and restored her to herself. Gladly did I pay the man the sum which had been promised him, and fortunately our finances were in safety, for Satyrus had our money about his person at the time when we were shipwrecked, and neither he nor Menelaus had been plundered by the buccaneers. While what I have been relating took place, a much more powerful force arrived from the seat of government, which succeeded in completely destroying the pirate settlement.

As the river was now freed from any dangers on the part of these marauders, we prepared to sail for Alexandria, accompanied by Chæreas, for whom we had conceived a friendship on account of the discovery which he had made to us about the potion. He was a native of the Isle of Pharos, and his calling that of a fisherman; he had served in a naval expedition against the buccaneers, and at its termination had been discharged. The river which, owing to the depredations of the pirates, had for a long time been deserted, was now crowded with vessels; and a pleasant thing it was to hear the songs of the sailors and the mirth of the passengers, and to see so many craft passing up and down. Our voyage was like a continuous festival, and the river itself seemed to be keeping holiday. I for the first time drank some of the Nile water, without any admixture of wine, being desirous to test its sweetness,— and wine, I may remark, always spoils the flavour of water. Having filled a transparent crystal glass, the liquid vied with, nay, surpassed it in brightness. It was sweet to the taste, and had an agreeable coldness, whereas some of the Grecian rivers are so very cold as to be injurious to the health. On this account the Egyptians have no fear in drinking its water, and stand in no need of wine. Their way of drinking struck me as being curious. They do not draw up the water in a bucket, neither do they use any other cup than that which Nature has supplied,—their hand; when any one is thirsty he stoops over the side of the vessel, and, receiving the water in the hollow of his hand, jerks it upwards with such dexterity, that it is received into the open mouth, and not a drop is lost.

The Nile produces another monster, more noted for strength than even the river-horse, I mean the crocodile. His shape is between that of a fish and a large animal. His length from head to tail is great, and out of proportion to his breadth; his skin is rough with scales; the surface of his back hard and of a black colour, while the belly is white. He has four legs, which bend in an oblique direction, like those of the land tortoise; his tail is long and thick, forming a solid mass, and differing from that of other animals in being the continuation of the spine, and therefore a constituent part of the body, and on the top it is set with sharp spines, like the teeth of a saw. It serves the crocodile for an implement with which to capture his prey; he strikes with it against his antagonist, and a single stroke will inflict several wounds. His head grows directly out of his shoulders in one line, for Nature has concealed his neck. The most formidable part about him are his jaws, which open to an immense extent; so long as they remain closed they form a head, but when expanded to take in its prey, they become all mouth; (the animal, I may observe, moves only the upper jaw) for so great is their expansion that it reaches to the shoulders and to the orifice of the stomach. He has many teeth, which are disposed in long rows: they are said to equal the days of the year in number. Were you to see the animal on land, you would not suppose him to be possessed of so much strength, judging from his size.

Book V

W e arrived at Alexandria after a three days' passage. I entered by
the gate of the Sun, and was at once amazed and delighted by
the splendour of the city. A row of columns, on either side, led in a
straight line to the gate of the Moon—these two divinities being the
guardian gods of the city gates. In the midst of these columns was the
open part of the city, which branched out into so many streets, that in
traversing them, one seemed journeying abroad though all the time at
home. Proceeding a little farther I came to a part named after the great
Alexander; here began a second city and its beauty was of a twofold
kind, two rows of columns equal in extent, intersecting each other at
right angles. It was impossible to satisfy the eye with gazing upon the
various streets, or to take in every object deserving of admiration; some
of these one actually saw, others one was on the point of seeing; others
one longed to see; others, again, one would not willingly have missed
seeing; those which were actually present rivetted one's gaze; those
which were anticipated tempted it to wander: after turning my eyes
therefore, on every side, so distracted were my feelings of admiration,
that I owned my sight to be thoroughly bewildered and unequal to
its task. What most struck me was the extent of the city and its vast
population, each of which in turn bore away the palm when compared
with the other; the former seemed actually a country, the latter, a nation.
When I looked at the vast size of the city, I doubted whether any number
of inhabitants could fill it; and when I considered the multitude of the
inhabitants, I asked myself whether any city could contain them; so
evenly balanced was the calculation, and so difficult was it to come to
a decision.

It chanced at that time to be the festival of the great deity called
Jove by the Greeks, Serapis by the Egyptians; torches were lighted up
throughout the city, and the effect of so much light was marvellous, for
although evening had come on and the sun had set, there was no such
thing as night, another sun might be said to have arisen, only that his
rays were scattered, so that the city vied with heaven in brightness. I
also visited the magnificent temple and saw the statue of the Milichian
Jove, and after paying our devotions to his great divinity, and praying
him to end at last, our troubles, we returned to the lodgings which
Menelaus had engaged for us. The deity, as will be seen, did not hearken

to our prayers, and another trial of fortune yet awaited us. Chæreas had for some time been enamoured of Leucippe, which was his motive for communicating to me the circumstance of the philtre, by doing which he hoped to become on intimate terms with us and to preserve her life for his own ends. Knowing how difficult success would be, he had recourse to stratagem. Being a seafaring man, he had no difficulty in getting together some fellows, half-fishermen half-pirates, with whom he arranged what was to be done, and then under pretence of keeping his birth-day, he invited us to an entertainment at Pharos. As we were leaving the house a sinister omen befell us; a hawk pursuing a sparrow struck Leucippe on the cheek with its wing; alarmed at the occurrence I looked up towards heaven and said—"Jove, what means this omen? If this bird be indeed sent by thee, show us, I pray, some clearer augury." Upon turning round, I found myself standing by a painter's shop where was a picture, the subject of which was in keeping with what had just taken place; it represented the rape of Philomela, the cruelty of Tereus in cutting out her tongue, every particular of the sad drama was seen depicted on the tapestry, which was being held up by a female slave. Philomela stood pointing to the different figures which were worked upon it, and Procne was intimating that she understood her, at the same time casting stern and angry looks upon the picture. There, the Thracian Tereus was seen struggling with Philomela, whose hair was dishevelled, her girdle loose, her dress torn, her bosom half naked; her right hand was planted against the face of Tereus, with her left she was endeavouring to pull her torn dress over her breast; Tereus was holding her in his arms, drawing her person towards him, and embracing her as closely as he could. Such was the subject of the tapestry. In the remainder of the painting, were seen the two sisters showing Tereus the relics of his supper, the head and hands of his own child; fear and bitter laughter are depicted on their faces; Tereus is leaping up from his couch and drawing his sword against them, and he has struck out his foot against the table which neither stands nor falls, but seems in the very act of falling. "In my opinion," said Menelaus, "we should give up the excursion to Pharos, for we have encountered two unfavourable omens, the hawk's wing and the threatening picture; now those who profess to interpret such matters, bid us pay regard to the subjects of any pictures which we may happen to meet with, when setting out on any business, and to conjecture the result of our undertaking from the nature of what we see. Did you not observe how full of evil augury this picture is? There is depicted in it lawless love, shameless adultery and female misery; we ought therefore to defer our expedition." I concurred in opinion with him, and we excused ourselves from accompanying Chæreas on that occasion; he left us, very much vexed at our determination, saying he should come to us the next day.

Women are naturally fond of hearing stories, accordingly when he was gone, Leucippe turning to me said, "Pray tell me what is the subject represented in this picture? What birds are they? who are the women? and who is that shameless man?" I proceeded to gratify her wishes.— "The hoopoe," I said, "was once a man called Tereus, the swallow and the nightingale were two sisters named Philomela and Procne, natives of Athens. One woman, it seems, is not enough for a barbarian, especially when an occasion offers for gratifying his lust; and such an opportunity was offered to Tereus through the sisterly affection of Procne, who sent her husband to invite Philomela; he conceived a passion for her, on his way back, made her a second Procne; then fearing lest she should reveal the deed, he, as the reward for her virginity deprives her of speech by cutting out her tongue, our nature's glory. The precaution was fruitless, Philomela, by her skill contrived a silent voice; she inwove the tragedy into a web, descriptive of the facts, her hand supplying the place of a tongue, and revealing to her sister's eyes what otherwise would have been whispered into her ears. Procne, learning through this device the violence which had been perpetrated, determines to take fearful vengeance; and two angry women's minds, conspiring together, and influenced by mingled feeling of jealousy and sense of wrong, contrive a supper more detestable even then the rape. They serve up to the father his own child; Procne had once been his mother, now she had forgotten the maternal tie, so powerfully do the pangs of jealousy prevail over those even of travail; for women, when exacting satisfaction for a violated bed, however deeply they may suffer in what they do, compensate the pain by the pleasure of inflicting vengeance. Tereus supped upon this hellish banquet, and afterwards the sisters, trembling with fear yet laughing horribly, bringing the remnants of his child upon a dish. He recognizes the miserable tokens, curses the food which he had swallowed, and discovers himself to be the father of what he had been feasting on. Maddened with fury, he draws his sword, and is in the act of rushing upon the women, when lo! the air receives them metamorphosed into birds. Tereus also becomes a bird, and ascends after them; and to show that their change of form has wrought no change in their hate, the hoopoe (Tereus) still pursues, and the nightingale (Procne) still flies." We had for once escaped the snare laid for us, but we gained by it only a single day, for next morning Chæreas arrived, and feeling ashamed to make any more excuses we went on board a vessel and sailed to Pharos. Menelaus said that he felt indisposed and remained at home. Chæreas took us first to the light-house and directed our attention to the wonderful superstructure upon which it stood—a rock situated in the sea, almost cloud-capped, and seeming to hang over the waters; upon the summit of this arose the tower, which with its light served vessels for a second pilot. When we had viewed this, he took us to a house at the extremity of the isle and situated on the shore.

In the evening, under pretence of his stomach being disordered, he went out: in a short time we heard a great noise, and suddenly a number of powerful men burst into the room, sword in hand, and turned towards the maiden. Seeing my dearest life about to be carried off, I rushed into the midst of them armed as they were, and received a wound in the thigh, from the effect of which I fell bathed in blood; they immediately put Leucippe into a boat and rowed away. Aroused by the disturbance and alarm caused by this occurrence, the commandant of the isle came up whom I had known when with the army. I exhibited my wound, and earnestly besought him to pursue the pirates. Accordingly, throwing himself and the soldiers with him into one of the many boats which were in the harbour, he gave them chase; I likewise was among the number, having caused myself to be lifted in.

When the pirates saw that we were gaining upon them and were prepared for an attack, they placed the maiden upon the deck with her hands bound behind her; some of them, after calling out in a loud voice, "Behold the prize you wish to win," severed her head from her body, and threw the trunk into the sea. Upon beholding this I uttered a loud cry and was on the point of casting myself into the water, but was prevented by those standing near me; I then requested the crew to lie upon their oars, that some one might jump into the sea and if possible recover the body for burial; they complied with my request and two of the sailors throwing themselves over the boat's side, got hold of the corpse and brought it on board. Meanwhile the pirates plied their oars still more vigorously, and when we were again nearing them they caught sight of another vessel, and recognizing those in her, hailed them to come to their assistance; these latter were purple-fishers and like the others pirates. The commandant, seeing the odds against him, became alarmed and gave orders to back water, for the pirates instead of continuing their flight, were now eager to provoke an engagement. Upon reaching the shore and landing, I threw myself upon the body and shed bitter tears.—"Thou hast indeed died a double death, my dearest Leucippe," I exclaimed, "divided as thou art between land and sea; I have a remnant of thee, but thou thyself art lost to me; the division is unfair, for thy larger portion which I possess (thy body) is in reality, thy lesser, (considering its worth,) while the sea, in retaining the lesser part (thy head), is in fact guilty of retaining all; since cruel Fortune envies me the happiness of kissing thy fair face, I will at least kiss thy neck." After giving vent to these lamentations, I had the body interred, and returned to Alexandria, where much against my will my wound was dressed, and where I continued to live a miserable life, though Menelaus did all in his power to console me. At the expiration of six months, the violence of my grief began to subside; time acts as medicine upon sorrow and heals the wounds which have been inflicted upon the soul, for the light of day, and the bright sun are full of cheerfulness, and though the mind may be fevered by excess of sorrow for a time, yet it is gradually cooled and overcome by the persuasive influence of time.

One day, when walking in the public square, some one came behind me, and without speaking a word, seized my hand, turned me round, and warmly embraced me. For a few moments I knew not who the party was, overcome by surprise I mechanically suffered myself to be embraced; at length, upon looking up and seeing his features, who should it prove to be but Clinias, so uttering a cry of joy, I returned his embrace with ardour. We then retired to my lodging, where I told him the particulars of Leucippe's death, and he related to me the manner of his escape.—"When the ship went to pieces," said he, "I laid hold of one end of the sailyard, which was already crowded with people, and endeavoured to hang on; after we had been tossed about for some time, a great wave overtaking us raised and dashed the yard against a sunken rock, from which it rebounded like an engine, and shot me off as though I had been hurled from a sling. I swam during the rest of the day, but with little hope of being saved; at length, when exhausted and abandoning myself to the will of Fortune, I espied a vessel bearing down towards me; so alternately lifting up my hands, I supplicated help by gestures. Moved by pity, or perhaps merely obeying the impulse of the wind, the ship came near me, and while running by, one of the sailors cast a rope over the side; I seized it, and was thus drawn out of the jaws of death. The vessel was bound for Sidon, and some of those on board to whom I was known showed me every kindness. We arrived at the above city after two days' sail, when I requested the Sidonians on board (the merchant Xenodamas, and his father-in-law Theophilus), not to mention to any of the Tyrians whom they might meet, the circumstance of my being preserved from shipwreck. I did not wish any one to know that I had been away from home, and if those two preserved silence in the matter, I had hopes that nothing would be discovered; five days only had elapsed since my disappearance, whereas if you recollect, I had told my servants that I was going into the country for ten days; and fortunately I found this to be the prevalent belief among my friends. Your father did not return home until two days after this, upon his arrival he found a letter from his brother, Sostratus (which came the very day after our departure), in which he offered you his daughter's hand. Upon reading it and hearing of our flight your father was in great trouble, both because you had missed the prize intended for you, and because after so nearly bringing matters to a favourable issue, Fortune had failed merely through delay in the arrival of the letter. Not wishing his brother to know what had happened, he enjoined secrecy upon Leucippe's mother, thinking it probable he should be able to discover you, or at any rate, that upon hearing of the betrothment, you would both gladly return, having it in your power to realize the object of your flight. He is now using every endeavour to find you out; and only a few days ago, Diophantus of Tyre, just returned from Egypt, informed him that he had seen you here; immediately upon hearing this, I took ship, sailed hither, and have for more than a week been seeking you in this city. As your father will soon be here, it is time for you to decide upon some plan." He ceased speaking, and I could not help inveighing bitterly against the cruel sport of Fortune. "How unfortunate is my lot, my uncle Sostratus gives me the hand of Leucippe, and sends me a bride from the theatre of war, so exactly measuring the time as to avoid anticipating our flight. My good luck and happiness comes just one day too late! Marriage and the nuptial hymn is talked of when death has claimed his victim, and it is a time for tears! Whom do they now offer me for a bride? Even her whose corpse I am not permitted to possess entire!" "You have no leisure for lamentations now," said Clinias; "what you have to settle is, whether you will return to your own country or await your father's arrival here."—"I will do neither the one nor the other," I replied; "how can I look my father in the face, after basely flying from his house, and enticing away her whom his own brother had entrusted to his charge? Nothing remains but to quit this city before he comes." At this moment Menelaus came in, accompanied by Satyrus, and upon seeing Clinias they hastened to embrace him. When informed by us of the state of affairs,—"You have an opportunity," said Satyrus, "of prosperously settling all your affairs, and of taking pity upon a heart which burns with love towards you. Listen," continued he, addressing Clinias, "Venus has thrown a piece of good fortune in the way of Clitopho which he is unwilling to accept; a lady, by name Melitta, a native of Ephesus is doatingly in love with him; so rare is her beauty, that it fits her for a sculptor's model. She is rich and young, and has lately lost her husband who was drowned at sea; she earnestly desires to make Clitopho, I will not say merely her husband but her 'lord paramount,' and freely surrenders to him herself and all she has. She has passed two whole months here, endeavouring to persuade him. Yet he, heaven knows why, looks coldly upon her, and slights her suit, imagining, I suppose, that Leucippe will come to life again."

"In my opinion," replied Clinias, "Satyrus speaks sensibly; it is no time for hesitation and delay, when beauty, health, wealth, and love combine to woo you; her beauty will yield you delight, her wealth will supply the means of luxurious enjoyment, and her love will gain consideration for you; consider, moreover, that the deity hates pride and arrogance, so follow the advice of Satyrus and yield to destiny."— "Well then," said I, with a deep sigh, "do with me what you will, since Clinias is of your opinion; one stipulation I make, however, that I am not to be pressed to consummate the marriage until we arrive at Ephesus, for I have taken a solemn oath to be connected with no woman in this city where I have been bereaved of my Leucippe." Upon hearing me say this, Satyrus hastened to Melitta with the joyful tidings, and shortly after returned and said, that upon learning them, she had nearly fainted from excess of joy; he was also the bearer of an invitation to me to come to supper as a prelude to the marriage. I complied and proceeded to her house. No sooner did she see me, than falling on my neck she covered me with kisses. I must do her the justice of saying that she was really beautiful; her complexion was fair as milk, but tinted with the rose, her bright and sunny look was worthy of Venus herself, and she had a profusion of long golden hair, so that upon the whole I could not look at her without some pleasurable emotions.

A costly supper was served, she now and then took some of the viands for appearance sake, but in reality ate nothing, feeding her eyes on me. Lovers find their chief delight in gazing upon the beloved; and when once this tender passion has taken possession of the soul, there is no time or desire for taking food. The pleasure conceived by the eyes flows through them into the mind, bears along with it the image of the beloved, and impresses its form upon the mirror of the soul; the emanation of beauty darting like secret rays and leaving its outline on the love-sick heart. I said to her, "Why is it that you touch none of your own delicacies?—you are like one of those who sup on the painter's canvas."—"The sight of you," replied she, "is more to me, than the choicest viands and the richest wines," accompanying the words with one of her kisses which I began to receive with some degree of pleasure; "this," said she after a pause, "is meat and drink to me."

In this manner did supper pass; at night she used every endeavour to persuade me to remain and share her bed; I however excused myself urging the same reason which I had previously advanced to Satyrus. Much against her will she allowed me to depart, upon the understanding that next day we should meet in the temple of Isis, in order to arrange matters and to plight our troth in presence of the goddess; accordingly I went thither the following morning accompanied by Clinias and Menelaus, and we took a mutual oath, I to love her in all sincerity; she, to take me for her husband and to give me the control of all her property. I reminded her that the performance of these promises was to be deferred until we should arrive at Ephesus, "for as long as we are here," I said, "you must give place to my Leucippe." Another magnificent banquet was prepared, which was in name but not in reality the marriage supper, for as I have said, the consummation of our nuptials was postponed. During the entertainment, when the guests were wishing heath and happiness to the new married pair, Melitta turning to me, said half in jest, half in earnest, "How flat, stale, and unprofitable is all this, like the empty honours sometimes bestowed upon the dead; I have often heard of a tomb without a body, but never till now of a wedding without a consummation." The next morning, induced by a favourable wind, we sailed from Alexandria; Menelaus accompanied us to the port, and after many embraces and wishes for my having a more prosperous voyage than formerly, took his leave; he was in all respects a worthy and excellent young man, and we mutually shed tears at parting. Clinias would not leave me, but determined to accompany us as far as Ephesus, and after remaining there some time, to return, as soon as my affairs were comfortably settled. The wind continued in our favour the whole day, and at night after supper we retired to rest in a cabin which had been parted off for me and Melitta in the hull of the vessel. We had no sooner entered it, then throwing her arms around me she urged me to consummate our marriage. "We are now," she said, "beyond the boundaries sacred to Leucippe, and within those where you are pledged to perform your promise. What need is there to delay until we arrive at Ephesus? Remember, the sea is not to be depended on, the winds are faithless! Believe me, Clitopho, I burn; would that I should actually show the intenseness of the fire! would that it possessed the same nature as the ordinary fires of love; that so I might inflame you by my embraces! but, alas! it has a nature peculiar to itself, and the flame which usually extends its influence to both the lovers, in my case burns only its possessor! Strange and mystic fire, which refuses to quit its own peculiar precints; dearest Clitopho, let us begin the rites of Venus!"—"Do not," I replied, "urge me to forget that reverence which is due to the departed; we cannot be said to have passed the limits sacred to her memory until we arrive in another country. Have you not heard how she perished in the sea? I am therefore still sailing over Leucippe's grave; nay more, her shade may even now be flitting around our vessel: it is said that the souls of those who have found a watery grave do not descend to Hades, but wander about the surface of the waves; for aught we know, she may appear to us in the midst of our embrace. Besides, can you consider the tossing waves of the uncertain sea, a fitting place for consummating a bridal? Would you wish to have a fluctuating and unstable marriage bed?"—"Dearest," she resumed, "lovers need no feather-bed, every place is accessible to the god of love; nay, rather is the sea a most proper and fitting place for celebrating the mysteries of Venus. Is not that goddess daughter of the sea: in honouring her shall we not be paying homage to her mother? Everything around us, moreover, is emblematic of the marriage rites; above us is the sailyard (resembling in form a yoke) encircled by its ropes;—what can more fitly symbolise a wedding than a yoke and bands? close to our bed is the rudder, emblem of safe arrival within the port; Fortune herself is clearly guiding our nuptials to a happy issue. Neptune himself, who wedded a sea-bride, will wait upon us with his choir of Nereids; and the winds which sigh so softly among the ropes seem to be chanting our nuptial song; look too, at the bellying canvas, how it resembles a pregnant womb; even this is not without its propitious meaning, for it tells me that ere long you will be a father!"

Seeing her become so pressing and so excited, I replied,—"Let us, if you will, continue to discuss these subtle points until we reach our destination; I swear to you by the sea itself and by the fortune of our voyage, that I am as impatient as yourself; but remember that even the sea has its peculiar laws; and I have often heard say from ancient mariners that ships must not be made the scenes of amorous delights, either as being sacred in themselves, or because wanton pleasure is unseemly amid the perils of the ocean. Let us not then, my love, cast insult upon the sea, or cause our nuptials to be distracted by alarms, rather let us keep in store for ourselves pure and unalloyed delight." These arguments mingled with kisses and endearments, produced the desired effect; and we passed the remainder of the night in sleep. Five days more, brought us to Ephesus; Melitta's house was one of the finest in the city, it was spacious and handsomely furnished, and she had a numerous establishment. After ordering a handsome supper she proposed that we should in the meanwhile visit her country-house, which was not more than half a mile out of town; we rode there in her carriage, and then getting out walked about in the kitchen-garden. Suddenly a female approached and threw herself at Melitta's feet; she had on heavy fetters and held in her hand a hoe, her hair had been cut off, her whole appearance was squalid, and her clothing consisted of a sorry tunic. "Lady," she exclaimed, "have pity upon one of your own sex, who once was free, but is now by the caprice of Fortune, a slave."—"Rise up," replied Melitta, "and tell me who you are and from whence you came, and by whom you have been thus fettered; for though in rags and misery your countenance bespeaks good birth."—"I received this treatment from your bailiff," resumed the woman, "because I refused to gratify his desires; my name is Lacæna and I am from Thessaly; I throw myself upon your mercy, beseeching you to release me from this wretched condition, and to guarantee my safety till I shall have paid the two thousand drachmas, for which Sosthenes purchased me from the hands of pirates; the sum shall soon be raised, and until then I am willing to remain your slave. See," she continued, "how cruelly I have been used," and opening her tunic she shewed her back furrowed with stripes, a pitiable sight. Her voice and appearance overwhelmed me with strange feelings, for I seemed to recognize in her a resemblance to Leucippe. Addressing her, "Be comforted," said Melitta, "I will have you set at liberty and will send you home without ransom,"—then speaking to a slave, "Summon here Sosthenes!" The unhappy woman was then disincumbered of her fetters, and the steward made his appearance in great trepidation.—"Villain," said Melitta, "did you ever see any one, even among the most ill-conditioned of my slaves, used so shamefully?— tell me instantly, without any shuffling, who this female is."

"Mistress," replied the fellow, "all I know is, that a merchant, called Callisthenes, sold her to me, saying that he had bought her from some pirates, that she was free-born, and named Lacæna." Melitta instantly degraded him from his office, but her she entrusted to the charge of her maid-servants, with orders to have her washed, decently dressed, and conducted to the city; then, after settling the business which had brought her thither, we rode back, and sat down to supper. While we were thus employed, Satyrus with a very serious countenance motioned to me to come out of the room: I did so, making some trifling excuse, when without uttering a word he put into my hand a letter, which even before reading it, filled me with consternation, for I recognized Leucippe's writing;—the contents were these:—

"Leucippe, to my master Clitopho.

"I am in duty bound to address you by this title, since you are united in marriage to my mistress. Although you are well aware of my sufferings on your account, it is necessary for me to remind you of them. For you I left the protection of my mother and became a wanderer; for you I suffered shipwreck and endured captivity among pirates; for you I became an expiatory victim and underwent a second death; for you I have been sold to slavery, bound in letters, made to bear a mattock and to hoe the ground; for you I have been beaten with the scourge;—and all this in order that you might become wedded to another woman—for suppose not that I will give myself up to any other man. No! I have borne, and without a murmur, all these ills, and you, exempt from them, have been enabled to form new marriage ties; if therefore you are impressed with any sense of the sufferings which I have undergone for love of you, urge your wife to send me home in accordance with her promise, and undertake to be security for the payment of the two thousand drachmas, which on my return, as I shall not be far from Byzantium, I will procure and send; though supposing you should have to pay them out of your own purse, it will only be a trifling compensation for all that I have suffered in jour behalf. Farewell, and may happiness attend your marriage—and remember that she who writes this letter has preserved her honour undefiled."

Upon reading these lines, I became a prey to a succession of conflicting feelings; love, fear, astonishment, doubt, joy, grief, by turns took possession of my mind.

"Did you bring this letter from the Shades below," I inquired of Satyrus. "What in the name of heaven does all this mean? Has Leucippe come to life again?"—"Most assuredly she has," replied he; "it is no other than she whom you saw in the country, but she is so changed in appearance from having had her hair cut off, that scarcely any one would recognize her."—"And are you going to stop short at this good news?" I asked: "Do you mean my ears alone to be gratified and my eyes to have no share in the delight?"—"For heaven's sake be cautious," was his reply; "let us first contrive some course of action, else you will bring destruction on us all. Only consider; here is this lady, one of the most distinguished for rank and wealth in Ephesus, madly in love with you, and we are in the midst of the toils without any possibility of getting free."—"Talk not of caution," rejoined I, "it is out of the question, joy thrills too strongly through all my veins. Think, too, how she upbraids me in her letter"—and upon this, I again eagerly ran over the contents, fancying I could see her in every line, and exclaiming as I read;—"Yes, dearest Leucippe, I plead guilty to thy charge! Thou hast indeed endured all these things for love of me! I have been the cause to thee of infinite misfortune!" And upon coming to the mention of the scourgings and other sufferings inflicted upon her by Sosthenes, I wept as though actually a witness of their infliction. Reflection turns the eyes of the soul upon the purport of what we read, and brings everything as vividly before us, as if it were actually being seen and done. Such was the influence of Leucippe's words, that her allusion to my marriage made me blush as though I had been really surprised in the commission of adultery.

"Satyrus," said I, "what excuses shall I offer? Leucippe, it is clear, knows everything; nay, her love may have become changed into hate! But tell me by what means she has been preserved? Whose corpse was that which was buried?"—"She will herself relate everything in proper season," he replied.—"What you have to do now is to write back an answer, in order to soothe her irritation. I solemnly declared to her that you married your present wife against your will."—"What! did you really tell her I was married? You have utterly undone me then! How could you be guilty of such folly?"—"Why tax me with folly? The whole city is aware of it."—"But I swear by Hercules and my present

Fortune that no actual marriage has taken place."—"Nonsense! you share her bed."—"I well know," said I, "that I shall not be credited, but nevertheless I speak the truth: up to this very day Clitopho has had no connexion with Melitta; however, the present question is, what am I to write to Leucippe? My mind is so confused by what has taken place, that I really know not how to begin."—"Upon my word," said Satyrus, "it is out of my power to help you, but I have no doubt that Love will suggest materials for a letter; but whatever you do, lose no time." I at length wrote as follows:—

"Health to Leucippe, mistress of my heart! It is my lot to be at once happy and unhappy;—happy in that I have you mentally present to me; unhappy in that you are really absent from me. Only defer pronouncing judgment upon me until the truth shall be cleared up, and you will find that the example of your chastity has been followed by myself (if chastity may be spoken of in men); but if you already hate and have condemned me unheard, I swear to you, by those gods who have preserved your life, that ere long you shall have proof of my perfect innocence. Farewell, dearest, and still give me a place in your affections!"

This letter I delivered to Satyrus, desiring him to say all he could in my favour to Leucippe. I then went back to supper full of joy, but not free from grief, well knowing that Melitta would not allow the night to pass without pressing me to consummate our nuptials, and, having recovered Leucippe, it was hateful to me even to look upon any other woman. I endeavoured to conceal what was passing in my mind, but it was to no purpose, so at last I feigned to be seized with a shivering fit.

Melitta guessed that I was seeking some excuse for not complying with her wishes, though as yet she had no actual proof. When, however, I arose from table without finishing my supper, and retired to rest, she got up and followed me into the bed-room. I then pretended that I felt much worse, upon which she became very urgent with me, and said, "Why will you persist in acting thus? How long will you continue to disappoint me? We have now crossed the sea, we are at Ephesus; the time is come for realizing your promise. Why should there be any more delay? How long are we to sleep together as though we were in a sanctuary? You place before my eyes a refreshing stream, of which nevertheless you prohibit me to drink; and though sleeping near the very fountain head, I am parched with thirst; my couch may compare with the feast of Tantalus." While thus venting her grief, she leaned her head upon my bosom and wept so piteously that I could not but sympathize with her sorrow; and feeling her reproaches to be just, I really was at a loss what to do. At last I said, "Believe me, dearest, by our country's gods, I feel an ardour equal to your own! but this sadden indisposition has seized me,—I know not from what cause,—and, as you are well aware, without the blessing of health it is in vain to think of love."

While saying this, I wiped away her tears, and solemnly assured her, that ere long she should obtain everything she wished. Not without great difficulty, however, did I succeed in pacifying her. On the following day Melitta called for the maid-servants, to whom she had committed Leucippe, and inquired whether every requisite attention had been shewn her. They replied, that nothing had been omitted. Upon this Melitta sent for her, and when she came into the room said, "I need scarcely remind you of the kindness you have experienced from me; all I ask as a return is assistance which it is in your power to afford me. Now, I understand that you Thessalian women can, by your magic, work so powerfully upon the minds of those you love, that their affections, instead of wandering to any other object, will thenceforth be wholly rivetted on you, their mistresses. It is a magic potion of this kind which I now want from you, to procure requital for the love which is consuming me. You remember, doubtlessly, the young man who was walking with me yesterday?"—"I suppose you mean your husband," replied Leucippe, maliciously, "for I have been told by some of the household that he stands to you in that relation."—"A pretty kind of husband!" interrupted Melitta; "he has in him more of marble than of manhood; and my rival is a certain dead Leucippe, whose name, whether waking or sleeping, is always on his lips. Four whole months have I spent in Alexandria, entirely on his account, praying and beseeching him, and leaving nothing undone likely to gain his love, but all to no purpose, for he remained as insensible to my entreaties as any stock or stone; and when at length he did give way, it was to become my husband but in name; for I swear to you by Venus, that after sleeping with him for a week I have risen from his side as if I had been sleeping with a eunuch; in short, I have fallen in love with a statue, not a man. To use the words, therefore, which yesterday you addressed to me, 'Have compassion upon one of your own sex;' give me your aid against the overweening and unimpressible man; by so doing you will save my life, which is now fast ebbing from me."

Leucippe was rejoiced at finding that no intercourse had taken place between Melitta and myself, and believing it to be of no use to deny her magic skill, undertook to find suitable herbs, if permitted to go and seek for them in the country. These promises tranquillized Melitta, for the mind is easily persuaded to feed upon the empty hope of future good. Meanwhile, knowing nothing of all this, I was in great perplexity how to put off Melitta during the approaching night, and to contrive a meeting with Leucippe. In the evening, Melitta, who had taken her out of town in a carriage, returned, and we had just began our supper when a great disturbance was heard in the men's quarter of the house, and a servant rushed into the room, out of breath, and exclaiming, "Thersander is alive, and is arrived!"

This Thersander was no other than Melitta's husband, who was supposed to have been lost at sea, the report of his death having been spread by two of his servants who had been saved when the ship was wrecked. In a moment he was in the room; for, having learnt every particular by the way, he had hastened home on purpose to surprise me. Melitta, in great alarm at an event so utterly unlooked for, started up and endeavoured to embrace her husband; who, however thrust her from him with great violence, and then catching sight of me and exclaiming, "So, here is the spark himself!" he rushed towards me, and dealt me a tremendous blow in the face, after which, seizing me by the hair, he dashed me to the ground and beat me most unmercifully. All this time I remained as silent as if I had been at the celebration of the mysteries, neither asking him who he was, or why he used me so; for, suspecting the truth, I had not courage to retaliate, though possessing physical strength enough to do so.

At length when he was weary of striking and I of forming conjectures in my mind, I got up and said, "Pray, who are you, and what do you mean by this rough usage?" More than ever irritated by the sound of my voice, he recommenced his attack upon me, and called aloud for fetters and handcuffs; they were brought, and, after being bound hand and foot, I was shut up in a room. During this struggle, Leucippe's letter, which had been fastened under my tunic to the fringes of my shirt, fell to the ground without my perceiving it, and was picked up by Melitta, who feared lest it might be one of her own letters written to me; when, however, she had an opportunity of reading it in private and met with Leucippe's name, it went like an arrow to her heart, but having so often heard of her death she did not at once identify the name with the female whom she had set at liberty; but as she read on, and felt all uncertainty upon the point removed, she became at once the divided prey of shame, rage, love, and jealousy;—she felt ashamed at exposure before her husband; she was enraged at the contents of the letter; this passion yielded to love on my account, which in its turn was stung by jealousy; but love, in the end, remained triumphant. Thersander, after the first ebullition of his anger, had retired to the house of a friend; Melitta, therefore, in the evening, after speaking to the slave who kept guard over my apartment, came in privately, having for precaution posted two of her servants before the door.

She found me lying upon the floor, and approaching me shewed by her countenance, that she wished, were it possible, to give utterance in one breath to all her various emotions. "Wretched that I am," she at length exclaimed, "fatal for me was the day when I first beheld you; I, who have loved so madly yet so fruitlessly; who still doat upon him who hates me; who pity him who is the cause of all my pain, and whose love is not extinguished even by injury and insult!—What a pair of juggling plotters against me are you both! You have all along been making me your sport, and she, forsooth, is gone to procure a philtre for me! Little did I dream that I was seeking aid from those who were my bitterest enemies!" Thus speaking she threw Leucippe's letter on the ground; which I no sooner recognized than a sudden chill came over me, and I cast my eyes upon the ground as if convicted of a crime. She then continued in the same strain: "What misery is mine! My husband is lost to me through you, and henceforth I shall be deprived even of the barren pleasure which I have enjoyed, that of seeing you! Through you I have incurred my husband's hatred, who believes me guilty of an intrigue against his honour—an intrigue which has borne me none of the fruits of love, and from which all I gain is infamy! Other women receive enjoyment for the guerdon of their shame: I inherit the shame, but obtain none of the enjoyment! Barbarous and faithless man, how can you allow a loving woman thus to pine away, when you are yourself the slave of Love? Did you not dread his anger? Had you no reverence for his fires,—no regard for his mysteries? Had these tearful eyes no influence over you,—more ruthless as you are than any pirate!—for even a pirate's breast will be softened by tears! Neither entreaty nor opportunity, nor my close embrace, has persuaded you to grant me so much as one amorous indulgence; nay, most insulting of all, after yourself returning my kisses and my embraces, you have risen from my side like any woman! What is this but the very ghost of matrimony? Remember also, that you have not been sharing the bed of one who is grown old, or who repulses your embraces, but of one who is young and ardent, and whom some might consider possessed of charms,—eunuch that you are!—unsexed and bane of beauty, listen to my righteous imprecation:—may Love requite your fires as you have requited mine!"

Tears for a time choked her voice; but when I remained still silent and with downcast eyes, a sudden change came over her, and she then resumed:—"Dearest Clitopho, anger and grief have hitherto dictated my words, but love prompts what I am now about to say; for believe me, however angry, I still burn with passion; however much wronged, I still feel love; yield to my entreaties then, and even now compassionate me! I no longer ask for joys of many days' duration, nor for the lengthened wedlock which in my folly I had dreamt of; I will be content with one amorous embrace. I ask but a little medicine to palliate this powerful disease,—extinguish, in some degree, the flame which now consumes me! Pardon me if I have spoken with too much haste and bitterness, for love when unsuccessful is pushed to phrenzy! Well aware how unseemly my conduct may appear, I am not ashamed to divulge the mysteries of Love, for I speak to one already initiated,—to one who knows by his own experience what my feelings are. Lovers alone understand the wounds felt by those who love; to all others the arrows of the god and the havoc which he makes are equally unknown. One only day remains to us. I ask the performance of your promise. Remember the temple of Isis; show regard to the oaths which you took there. Were you willing to live with me, according to the troth you plighted, I would not care for a thousand Thersanders; but having recovered your Leucippe, you may not wed another; accordingly I surrender every claim, and ask only what may easily be granted. It is vain to resist my destiny; all things evidently conspire against me,—even the dead rise up again. Cruel sea, thou hast borne me safely only to plunge me into greater ruin, bringing back to me, for my confusion, the very dead. Nor was it enough for Leucippe to revive in order to assuage the grief of Clitopho, but the savage Thersander also must needs come back. And he has dared to strike Clitopho before my eyes without my having the power to aid him; he has dared to disfigure that face upon which I doat. He must have been blind to beauty when he did so! Once more I entreat you, my Clitopho, lord, as you are, of my affections, give yourself to me now, for the first time and the last; it will be to me as if many days were crowded into one short space! so may you never more be deprived of your Leucippe; so may she never again die a fictitious death! Do not scorn my love; it has produced your greatest happiness; it has been the means of restoring to you Leucippe; had I never been enamoured of you, had I never brought you here, Leucippe would still be dead to you. Some thanks are due to good fortune, Clitopho; he who lights upon a treasure honours the spot where he discovered it; he builds an altar, he offers a sacrifice; he crowns the place with flowers; but though you have found in me a treasure full of love you despise your happy fortune! Think Love to be addressing you through my mouth, and saying, 'In this matter thou art bound to oblige me, thy tutor; initiate Melitta in my mysteries; I kindled the fire with which she burns.' Hear likewise how I have provided for your safety; you shall be set free from these chains, whether Thersander will or no, and you shall find a place of refuge with my foster-brother for as long a time as you may wish. In the morning you may expect to see Leucippe; she is to pass the night in the country for the sake of gathering herbs by moonlight, for my simplicity was so imposed upon, as to believe her a Thessalian, and to ask of her a philtre to be administered to you. What else could I do, when disappointed in my wishes, than have recourse to herbs and drugs, the refuge of those who are unfortunate in love. You need be in no fear of Thersander; he has rushed out of the house in a rage, and betaken himself to one of his friends. The deity, indeed, seems to have purposely contrived his absence, that I may obtain the last favour which I ask. Let me then enjoy you, Clitopho!"

After this earnest and impassioned pleading, suggested by Love, who is a mighty master of eloquence, she undid the fetters; and after kissing my hands applied them to her eyes and heart: "Feel," said she, "how my poor heart beats, agitated by fear and hope,—would that I could say, by pleasure!—and seeming to supplicate you by its palpitations." When, after setting me free, she hung about my neck in tears, I was no longer proof against human weakness; indeed I was in dread of incurring the wrath of Love himself, especially as I had now recovered Leucippe, and was about to leave Melitta, so that our present connexion would be no consummation of a marriage, but simply administering relief to a love-sick soul. Yielding to these reflections I returned her kisses and embraces, and though without the help of bed or other appliances of amorous delight, nothing was left to be desired. Love, indeed, is his own teacher, and an excellent contriver, and makes every place his temple; nor is there any doubt that impromptu amorous intercourse is far preferable to that which is elaborated, and that it brings with it much more genuine enjoyment.

Book VI

W hen at length, I had sufficiently eased Melitta's pains, I said to her, "How do you mean to provide for my escape and to perform your promises as to Leucippe?"—"Be in no anxiety respecting her," was the reply, "look upon her as already restored to your embrace; but put on my clothes and conceal your face in my robe; Melantho will conduct you to the door, there you will find a young man who has orders from me to guide you to the house where Clinias and Satyrus await you, and whither Leucippe will shortly come." While giving me these directions, she dressed me so as to resemble her in appearance; then kissing me, she said, "You look handsomer than ever in this attire, and remind me of a picture of Achilles which I once saw. Fare you well, dearest, preserve this dress as a memorial of me, and leave me your own, that I may sometimes put it on and fancy myself in your embrace;" she then gave me a hundred gold pieces, and called Melantho, a trusty servant, who was watching at the door, told her what to do, and ordered her to return, as soon as she had let me out. Thus disguised I slipped out of the room, the keeper, upon receiving a sign from Melantho, taking me for his mistress and making way; passing through an unfrequented part of the house I reached a back door, where I was received by the person whom Melitta had appointed to be there; he was a freedman who had accompanied us on our voyage from Alexandria, and with whom I had already been intimate.

Upon her return, Melantho found the keeper preparing to secure the room for the night, she desired him to open the door, and going in, informed her mistress of my escape; Melitta called in the keeper, who seeing the right bird flown and another in his place, was struck dumb with astonishment: "I did not employ this artifice," said she, "from believing you unwilling to favour Clitopho's escape, but because I wished to give you the means of clearing yourself from blame in the opinion of Thersander. Here are ten gold pieces; if you choose to remain here, you are to regard them as a present from Clitopho, if you prefer getting out of the way they will help you on your journey." "Mistress," replied the keeper, whose name was Pasio, "I am ready to follow your suggestion." It was agreed, that the man should go away and remain in concealment until Thersander's anger had subsided, and he and his wife were again upon good terms. Upon leaving the house, my usual ill fortune overtook me; and interwove a new incident in the drama of my life. Whom should I encounter but Thersander! who persuaded by his friend not to sleep away from his wife, was returning home.

It happened to be the festival of Diana, the streets were full of drunken fellows, and all night long crowds of people continued traversing the public square. I had hoped to encounter no other danger but this, but I was mistaken, peril of a worse kind was still in store for me. Sosthenes, the purchaser of Leucippe, whom Melitta had turned out of his office, no sooner heard of his master's return, than he not only continued to act as bailiff, but determined to revenge himself upon Melitta. He began by informing against me, acquainting his master with all which had taken place; he then invented a very plausible story above Leucippe, for finding he could not enjoy her himself he determined to play pimp to his master, and by that means to alienate him from his wife.—"Master," said he, "I have purchased a maiden of incredible beauty; words will not do her justice, to form a just idea of her you must see her; I have been keeping her purposely for you; for I heard that you were alive and fully believed the fact, but did not choose to make it public, in order that you might have clear proof of my mistress's guilt, and not be made the laughing stock of a foreigner and worthless libertine; my mistress took her out of my hands yesterday and thinks of giving her her freedom, but Fortune has reserved for you the possession of this rare beauty; she has been sent for some reason or other into the country, where she now remains, and where with your leave I will secure her until your arrival."

Thersander approved of his scheme and bid him put it into execution; accordingly Sosthenes proceeded to the farm, and finding out the cottage where Leucippe was to pass the night, he ordered two of the labourers to entice away the maids, who had accompanied her, under pretence of having something to say to them in private; he then went accompanied by two others, to the cottage where Leucippe was now alone, seized her and having stopped her mouth, carried her off to a lone habitation, where setting her down, he said, "Maiden, I am the bearer of great good fortune to you, and I hope that you will not forget me, in your prosperity; be under no alarm at having been carried off, no injury is intended you, it will be the means of obtaining my master for your admirer." Leucippe could not utter a word, so much was she overcome by the sense of the unexpected calamity. Sosthenes hurrying back informed Thersander of what he had done, again, extolling Leucippe's beauty to the skies; he was on the point of returning home, but inflamed by the description, and having his mind filled with such a lovely vision, he determined at once to pay a visit to the maiden as the festival was still on foot, and the distance not more than half a mile. It was when on his way thither, that disguised in Melitta's dress I came directly upon him. Sosthenes was the first to recognize me; "Here comes the rake-hell himself," exclaimed he, "masquerading it, in my mistress's clothes!"

The young man, my guide, who was a little in advance hearing this, took to his heels in a fright without giving me any previous warning. I was immediately seized by the pair, and the noise made by Thersander drew together a number of the revellers, when he became louder than ever in his charges, heaping upon me all manner of abuse, calling me a lecher, a cut-purse, and I know not what besides; in the end I was dragged to the public prison, thrust in, and a charge of *Crim. Con.* entered against me. The disgrace of a prison and the abuse gave me little or no concern, for as my marriage with Melitta had been public, I felt confident of being able to refute the charge of adultery; all my anxiety arose from not having actually recovered my Leucippe, for the mind is naturally inclined to be a "prophet of ill," our predictions of good are seldom realized. In the present case I augured nothing favourable for Leucippe, and was a prey to fears and suspicions of every kind.

Thersander, after having had me locked up, continued on his way, and upon his arrival found Leucippe lying upon the ground and brooding over what Sosthenes had said. Grief and fear were plainly depicted upon her countenance; indeed I consider it quite a mistake to say that the mind is invisible, it may be seen distinctly reflected on the face as in a mirror; in seasons of happiness joy sparkles in the eyes; in the time of sorrow the countenance is overcast and reveals the inward feelings. A light was burning in the cottage; upon hearing the door open, Leucippe raised her eyes for a moment and then cast them down again. It is in the eyes that beauty has its seat, and Thersander having caught a momentary glimpse of the beauty which (rapid as lightning) flashed from hers, was at once on fire with love, and waited spell bound, in hopes of her raising them again; but when she continued to gaze upon the ground, he said, "Fair maiden, why waste the light of thine eyes upon the earth, why not look up and let them dart fresh light into mine?"

Upon hearing his voice, Leucippe burst into tears, and appeared even more charming than before, for tears give permanency and increased expression to the eyes, either rendering them more disagreeable, or improving them if pleasing, for in that case the dark iris, fading into a lighter hue, resembles, when moistened with tears, the head of a gently-bubbling fount; the white and black growing in brilliancy from the moisture which floats over the surface, assume the mingled shades of the violet and narcissus, and the eye appears as smiling through the tears which are confined within its lids. Such was the case with Leucippe; her tears made her appear beautiful even in grief; and if after trickling down they had congealed, the world would have seen a species of amber hitherto unknown. The sight of her charms, heightened as they were by her grief, inflamed Thersander; his own eyes filled with moisture. Tears naturally awaken feelings of compassion, especially a woman's tears, and the more so in proportion to the copiousness with which they fall; and when she who weeps is beautiful and he who beholds her is enamoured, he cannot avoid following her example; the magic of her charms, which is chiefly in her eyes, extends its influence to him; her beauty penetrates into his soul, her tears draw forth his own, he might dry them, but he purposely abstains from doing so, for he would fain have them attract the notice of the fair one; he even checks any motion of his eyelids, lest they should fall before the time, sympathetic tears being the strongest proof of love. This was the case with Thersander, he shed tears partly because grief has really in it something which is infectious, partly that he might appear to sympathize with Leucippe's sorrow. "Pay her every attention which her state of mind requires," said he in an under tone to Sosthenes; "however unwillingly I will leave her for the present for fear of annoying her; when she is more composed I will pay her another visit. Maiden," added he, addressing her, "cheer up, I will soon find means to dry those tears of yours;" and whispering to Sosthenes, "remember," said he, "that you promote my suit, and come to me to-morrow morning," with which words he left the cottage.

While these things were taking place, Melitta had lost no time in sending a young man into the country, who was to bid Leucippe return without delay, as she had no longer any need of ingredients for a philtre. Upon his arrival, he found the female servants in great trouble seeking for her everywhere, he therefore at once came back and informed his mistress of what had taken place. Melitta, upon learning that Leucippe had disappeared, and that I had been committed to prison, was thrown into violent agitation: though ignorant of the whole truth her suspicions fell upon Sosthenes, and being determined to ascertain by means of Thersander where Leucippe was, she had recourse to subtlety, combining with it a show of truth. Upon Thersander coming home and shouting out, "So you have got your paramour set free and have smuggled him out of the town;—why did you not accompany him? why stop here? why not take yourself off, and see how he looks now that he is in 'durance vile?'"—"What paramour?" replied Melitta with the greatest composure. "What delusion are you labouring under?— If you will only calm your passion and listen to me, I will very soon explain the truth; all I wish for on your part, is candour; forget any slanderous reports which you have heard, let reason take the place of anger and listen to what I have to say.—This young man is neither my paramour nor yet my husband; he is a native of Phœnicia, and belongs to one of the first families in Tyre; he was so unfortunate as to suffer shipwreck and lost everything which he possessed. Upon hearing of his misfortunes I took compassion upon him (remembering what had befallen you), and received him into my house.

"'Thersander,' said I, mentally, 'may perhaps be wandering about himself, some tender hearted female may have taken pity upon him; nay, if as report says, he has perished, I will shew kindness to all who have experienced the perils of the sea!' Many are the shipwrecked passengers to whom I have shewn hospitality, to many a corpse washed up by the waves have I here given burial; if I saw so much as a plank from a vessel borne to land, I drew it up on shore, 'for,' I said, 'it may have belonged to the ship in which Thersander sailed!' This young man was one of the last who was rescued from a watery grave, and in treating him with kindness, I was in fact honouring you. Like you, dearest, he had encountered the perils of the deep; in him therefore, I was paying regard to the impersonation of your sufferings. You have now had laid before you the motives by which I have been influenced.—I may add, that he was in great sorrow for his wife; he had believed her dead, but she was still alive, and, as he was informed, in the power of Sosthenes our bailiff. The report proved true, for upon proceeding into the country we found her there. It is in your power to test the truth of what I say, you can bring before you both Sosthenes and the female of whom I speak; if you can convict me of falsehood, then call me an adultress." Melitta spoke, all along, as if in ignorance of Leucippe's disappearance, reserving to herself the power—should Thersander wish to ascertain the truth—of bringing forward the maid-servants who had accompanied Leucippe, and who could solemnly declare that the maiden was nowhere to be found. Her motive was to persuade Thersander of her own innocence, and it was for this purpose that she urged him to bring forward Leucippe. To give yet greater colour to her artful words, "Dearest husband," she added, "during the time that we lived together, you have never discovered any blot in my character, neither shall you do so now. The report, at present raised against me, has arisen from people being ignorant of the cause which induced me to shew kindness to this young man; rumour has been busy in your case, also; for you, recollect, were reported to have perished. Now rumour and calumny are two kindred evils, and the former may be called the daughter of the latter. Calumny is sharper than any sword—more burning than any fire, more pernicious than any Siren, while rumour is more fluid than water, swifter than the wind, fleeter than any wing of bird. No sooner has calumny shot forth a poisoned word than it flies like an arrow and wounds, even in his absence, him against whom it is directed; while whosoever hears this word is readily persuaded, feels his anger kindled, and turns all its violence against the victim. On the other hand, rumour the offspring of this shot, flows onward like a torrent, and floods the ears of every listener; words, like wind, speeding it on its course, and,—to use another similitude—the wings of the human tongue bearing it aloft and enabling it to cleave the air. These are the foes against whom I have to contend, they have gained the mastery over your mind, and have closed your ears against my words." Here she paused, and taking his hand endeavoured to kiss it; her plan was not without success, for Thersander became more calm, influenced by the plausibility of her speech, and finding the account given of Leucippe to harmonize with what he had heard from Sosthenes. His suspicions gave way, however, only in part, for jealousy when once it has gained entrance into the mind, is hard to be got rid of. The intelligence that the maiden was my wife annoyed him greatly, and increased his animosity towards me; and saying that he should enquire into the truth of what he had heard, he retired to rest alone.—Melitta, on her part was very much distressed at being unable to perform her promise. Meanwhile Sosthenes after the departure of Thersander (whom he had encouraged with hopes of speedy success) again went in to Leucippe, and assuming a joyful countenance, "Everything is going on satisfactorily Lacæna," said he, "Thersander is deeply enamoured of you, and very probably will make you his wife; this success is entirely owing to me, for I have extolled your beauty to the skies, and his mind sees and thinks of you alone. Dry your tears therefore, maiden, rise from the ground, sacrifice to Venus on account of your good fortune, and do not forget how much you owe to me." "May as much happiness befall you as you have just announced to me," was her reply. Sosthenes, believing that she spoke sincerely and not in irony, proceeded in a friendly tone and manner: "I will tell you moreover who Thersander is; he is the husband of Melitta whom you lately saw, his family is one of the first in Ionia, his wealth is even greater than his birth, but it is surpassed by his kindness of disposition. I need not dwell upon his age, for you have seen that he is still young and handsome, two qualities especially acceptable to women."

Leucippe could no longer endure listening to such nonsense: "Wicked wretch!" she exclaimed, "how much longer do you mean to pollute my ears? What is Thersander to me? Let his beauty delight his wife, his riches benefit his country, and his good qualities be of service to those who need them. What matters it to me, if he be nobler in birth than Codrus, and surpass Crœsus in his wealth? For what purpose should you enumerate another man's good qualities to me? Thersander shall receive my praise, when he ceases wishing to do violence to another's wife." Upon this, changing to a serious air, "Are you jesting, maiden?" he asked. "What have I to do with jesting?" was her reply. "Leave me to my own adverse fortune and evil genius; I know full well that I have fallen into the power of villains." "You must be incurably crazed," said Sosthenes, "to talk thus. Is it like being in the power of villains, to have the offer made to you of wealth, marriage, and a luxurious life; to receive for your husband one so favoured by the gods, that they have actually snatched him from the jaws of death?" And then he gave an account of the shipwreck, magnifying Thersander's escape, and making of it a greater wonder than of Arion and his Dolphin.

When he had finished his marvellous tale, and still Leucippe made no reply, "You had better consult your own interest," he resumed, "and not talk in this fashion to Thersander, lest you should provoke one who is actually amiable; for when once kindled, his anger knows no bounds. Kindness of heart, when it meets with a due return, increases, but when slighted, it soon changes into angry feelings; and then the desire of taking vengeance is proportioned to the previous willingness of doing good." Leaving Leucippe for a time, we will now speak of some of the other characters in this tale. When Clinias and Satyrus learned from Melitta that I had been incarcerated they immediately came to the prison, desirous of sharing my captivity; the jailor, however, would not consent, but bid them at once be gone, and though sorely disappointed there was no alternative. They left me, therefore, after I had enjoined them to bring me tidings of Leucippe in the morning; and I remained alone, thinking of Melitta's promise, and racked by feelings of mingled fear and hope.

The next day Sosthenes proceeded according to his appointment to Thersander, and my friends returned to me. Thersander eagerly inquired whether any favourable impression had been made upon Leucippe; Sosthenes replied evasively, "She raises objections against receiving you, but I scarcely believe her to be sincere in what she says; I rather suspect that she fears you may desert her and expose her to shame, after once enjoying her." "Let her dismiss all such apprehensions," replied Thersander; "my feelings of love towards her are so ardent, that they will end only with my life. One thing alone gives me uneasiness; I am very anxious to know for certain whether, as Melitta told me, she is the wife of the young man." Thus discoursing they came to the cottage where Leucippe was confined; when near the door they stopped and listened and could hear her speaking to herself in a mournful voice. "Alas! alas! Clitopho, you know not where I am and in what place I am detained; neither am I acquainted with your present condition; and this mutual ignorance augments our mutual grief. Can Thersander have surprised you in his house? Can you have suffered any cruel treatment at his hands? Often have I longed to question Sosthenes about you, but I was at a loss what reason to assign; if I spoke of you as my husband, I feared that by provoking the resentment of Thersander, I might produce evil consequences to yourself; if I inquired after you as after a mere stranger, it might have been said why do women meddle with what in no way concerns them? Often has my tongue been on the point of speaking but has refused its office. Often have I ended by saying to myself, 'Dear Clitopho, faithful husband of thy Leucippe, thou who couldst share the couch of another woman, yet without enjoying her, though I, in my jealousy doubted thy fidelity, could I indeed behold thee again, after so long an interval, and yet not snatch a single kiss!' What if Thersander comes again to question me? Shall I throw off all disguise, and disclose the plain unvarnished truth? Suppose not, Thersander, that I am a sorry slave; I am daughter of the Byzantian Commandant, wife of one foremost in rank among the Tyrians. I am no Thessalian, neither am I called Lacæna. No! this is the invention of pirate violence; my very name has been stolen from me! I am in reality the wife of Clitopho, a native of Byzantium, the daughter of Sostratus and Panthea. But, alas! Thersander would give no credit to my words, or, if he did, my freedom of speech might be the cause of injury to my best beloved! What then? I will again assume the mask—and again my name shall be Lacæna!" Thersander, retiring a little from the door, said to Sosthenes, "Did you hear those words of hers, unworthy of belief, indeed, as to their tenour, but full of the spirit of love, and breathing grief and self reproach? This adulterous rival of mine supplants me everywhere; the villain must surely be a sorcerer; Melitta loves, Leucippe doats upon him;—would that I were Clitopho!"

"You must not show a faint heart, master," replied Sosthenes; "you should go in at once and plead your suit; she loves this worthless fellow, it is true; but only because she has received addresses from no one else; you have but to insinuate yourself into her good graces, and your superior personal appearance will speedily gain the day and banish him from her heart. A new lover soon drives out the old. Women love the individual while present and remember him when absent until another is found to take, his place; then he is soon blotted from their recollection." Thersander now felt emboldened, for one readily believes words which flatter with a prospect of success; and desire, by dwelling upon its object, is sure to beget sanguine hope. After waiting a short time therefore, that he might not seem to have overheard her works, he put on what he hoped would appear an engaging air, and entered the cottage.

The sight of Leucippe inflamed his mind; she appeared more charming then ever, and her presence acted as fuel to the fire of love which had been burning in his breast all night. He with difficulty restrained himself from at once folding her in his arms, and sitting down beside her, began to talk of various unconnected trifles, as lovers are wont to do when in the company of their mistresses. At such times the soul is centred upon the object of its love, reason no longer guides their speech, and the tongue mechanically utters words. In the course of his address, he put his arm round her neck with the view of kissing her, and she aware of his intention hung down her head upon her bosom; he used all his endeavours to raise her face, and she with equal perseverance continued to conceal it the more and more; when this mutual struggle had continued for some time, Thersander, under the influence of amorous obstinacy, slipped his left hand under her chin, and seizing her hair with his right, compelled her to raise her head. When at length, he gave over, either from succeeding in his object, or failing, or from being weary of the sport, Leucippe said to him indignantly, "Your conduct is unfitting and ungentlemanly, though fit enough for the slave Sosthenes; the master and his man are worthy of each other; but spare yourself any farther trouble, you will never succeed unless you become a second Clitopho."

Distracted between anger and desire, Thersander was at a loss what to do. These passions are like two fires in the soul; they differ in nature, but resemble each other in intensity; the former urges to hatred, the latter to love; the sources also of their respective flames are near to one another, anger having its seat in the heart, the liver being the abode of love. When, therefore, a person is attacked by these two passions, his soul becomes the scales in which the intensity of either flame is weighed. Each tries to depress its respective scale, and love, when it obtains its object is generally successful; but should it be slighted, then it summons its neighbour, anger, to its aid, and both of them combine their flame. When once anger has gained the mastery, and has driven love from its seat, being implacable by nature, instead of assisting it to gain its end, it rules like a tyrant, and will not allow it (however anxious) to become reconciled with its beloved. Pressed down by the weight of anger, love is no longer free, and vainly endeavours to recover its dominion, and so is compelled to hate what once it doated upon. But, again, when the tempest of anger has reached its height, and its fury has frothed away, it becomes weary from satiety, and its efforts cease; then love, armed by desire, revives, comes to the rescue, and attacks anger sleeping on his post; and calling to mind the injuries done to the beloved during its frenzy, it grieves and sues for pardon, and invites to reconciliation, and promises to make amends in future. If after this it meets with full success, then it continues to be all smiles and gentleness; but if again repulsed and scorned, then its old neighbour, anger, is once more called in, who revives his slumbering fires, and regains his former power. Thersander, so long as he was buoyed up with hopes of succeeding in his suit, had been Leucippe's humble servant; but when he found all his expectations dashed to the ground, love gave way to wrath, and he smote her upon the face. "Wretched slave!" he exclaimed, "I have heard your love-sick lamentations, and know all; instead of taking it as a compliment that I should speak to you, and regarding a kiss from your master as an honour, you must, forsooth, coquet and give yourself airs; for my part, I believe you to be a strumpet, for an adulterer is your love! However, since you refuse to accept me as a lover, you shall feel my power as a master."

Leucippe meekly replied, "Use me as harshly as you please; I will submit to everything except the loss of chastity," and turning to Sosthenes, "you can bear witness to my powers of endurance; for I have received at your hands harder measure even than this!" Ashamed at having his conduct brought to light, "This wench," said he, "deserves to be flayed with the scourge and to be put upon the rack, in order to teach her better manners towards her master."

"By all means follow his advice!" resumed Leucippe to Thersander, "he gives good counsel; do the worst which your malice can suggest;— extend my hands upon the wheel; bare my back to the scourge; burn my body in the fire; smite off my head with the sword; it will be a novel sight to see one weak woman contend against all your tortures, victorious against all! You brand Clitopho as an adulterer, and yet you yourself would commit adultery! Have you no reverence for your tutelary goddess Diana? Would you ravish a virgin in the very city sacred to a virgin? O goddess, why do not thy shafts avenge the insult?" "You a virgin forsooth!" replied Thersander, contemptuously; "you who passed whole days and nights among the pirates! Prythee were they eunuchs, or given only to platonic love, or were they blind?"—"Ask Sosthenes," said she, "whether or not I preserved my chastity against his attempts; none of the freebooters behaved to me so brutally as you have done; it is you who deserve the name of pirate, since you feel no shame in perpetrating deeds which they abstained from doing. You little think how your unblushing cruelty will redound hereafter to my praise; you may kill me in your fury, and my encomium will be this: 'Leucippe preserved her chastity despite of buccaneers, despite of Chæreas, despite of Sosthenes, and crown of all (for this would be but trifling commendation), she remained chaste despite even of Thersander, more lascivious than the most lustful pirate; and he who could not despoil her of her honour, robbed her of her life.' Again, therefore, I say, bring into action all your engines and implements of torture, and employ the aid of Sosthenes, your right trusty counsellor. I stand before you a feeble woman, naked and alone, having but one weapon of defence, my free spirit, which is proof against sword and fire and scourge. Burn me, if you will; you shall find that there be things over which even the fire is powerless!"

Book VII

The scornful reproaches of Leucippe stirred up a tumult of conflicting passions in Thersander's mind; he was incensed by her taunts, vexed at his ill success, and perplexed how to secure the accomplishment of his desires. Without saying another word he rushed out of the house to give vent to the storm and tempest of his soul. Shortly after, having conferred with Sosthenes, he went to the jailor, and endeavoured to persuade him to administer a dose of poison to me; this, however, the jailor refused to do, his predecessor having suffered death for taking off a prisoner in this manner. Failing in this, he obtained his consent to introduce a man (who was to pass for a criminal) into my cell, under pretence of wishing to extract some secrets out of me through him. The man had been previously tutored by Thersander, and was casually to introduce Leucippe's name, and to say that she had been murdered by the contrivance of Melitta. Thersander's object in persuading me of her death was to hinder me (in case I obtained a verdict of acquittal) from instituting any further search for her recovery, and the name of Melitta was introduced in order that, after learning Leucippe's death, I might not entertain any thoughts of marrying her, and so by settling at Ephesus might interrupt Thersander in the prosecution of his schemes, but on the contrary, might be induced to quit the city without delay, from hatred to Melitta for having contrived the death of my beloved.

As soon as this fellow came near me, he began to play his appointed part, and with a knavish groan exclaimed, "Alackaday! what a miserable thing is life! There is no keeping out of trouble! It stands a man in no stead to be honest! Some cross accident is sure to overtake him! Would I could have guessed the character of my fellow traveller, and what work he had been engaged in!" This, and much more of the same sort, he said speaking to himself, craftily endeavouring to attract my attention, and to make me inquire what it was that ailed him. He did not succeed, however, for I was sufficiently taken up with my own troubles, and he went on with his groans and exclamations. At length—for the unfortunate take pleasure in listening to another's griefs, finding in it a kind of medicine for their sorrows—one of the prisoners asked, "What trick has the jade Fortune been playing you? I suspect that, like myself, she has laid you up in limbo without deserving it." He then proceeded to tell his own story, giving an account of what had brought him into prison; and having finished, requested the other to favour him with the particulars of his own misfortune. He of course readily complied.

"I left the city yesterday," said he, "to go towards Smyrna, and had proceeded about half a mile, when I was joined by a young man out of the country. He saluted me, and after walking with me for a few minutes, inquired whither I was going. I told him, and he said that luckily his road lay in the same direction, so that we proceeded in company, and entered into conversation. Stopping at an inn, we ordered dinner, and presently four men came in and did the same. Instead of eating, however, they continued watching us, and making signs to one another. I plainly enough saw that we were the objects of their notice, but was wholly at a loss to understand the meaning of their gestures. My companion gradually turned very pale, left off eating, and at last began to tremble all over. Instantly they sprang up, seized, and bound us; one of them also dealt him a violent blow upon the face; upon which, as if he had been already on the rack, and even without a question being asked him he cried out, 'I admit having killed the girl! Melitta, Thersander's wife, hired me to do the deed, and gave me a hundred gold pieces for my trouble; here they are every one—take them for yourselves; and for heaven's sake let me off!'"

Upon hearing these names I started as if stung, and turning to him, "Who is Melitta?" I asked.—"She is a lady of the first rank in this city," was his reply. "She took a fancy to a young man, said to be a native of Tyre; he found a favourite wench of his (whom he had given up for lost), among the number of Melitta's slaves, and she, moved by jealousy, had the girl seized by the fellow whom ill luck made my fellow-traveller, and he, in obedience to Melitta's orders, has made away with her.—But to return to my own story. I, who had never seen the man before, nor had dealings with him of any kind, was dragged along with him, bound, as an accomplice in his crime; but what is harder than all, they had not gone far, before, for the sake of his hundred pieces, they let him go, but kept me in custody and carried me before the judge."

Upon hearing this chapter of accidents, I neither uttered a sound nor shed a tear, for both voice and tears refused their office, but a general trembling seized me, my heart sunk within me, and I felt as at the point of death. After a time, recovering in some degree from the stupor which his words had caused, "How did the ruffian despatch her?" I asked, "and what has become of her body?" But having now performed the business for which he was employed, by stimulating my curiosity, he became obstinately silent, and I could extract nothing more from him. In answer to my repeated questions, "Do you think," said he, at length, "that I had a hand in the murder? The man told me he had killed her; he said nothing of the place and manner of her death." Tears now came to my relief, and I gave full vent to my sorrow. It is with mental wounds as with bodily hurts; when one has been stricken in body some time elapses before the livid bruise, the result of the blow is seen; and so also any one who has been pierced by the sharp tusk of a boar, looks for the wound, but without immediately discovering it, owing to its being deeply seated; but presently a white line is perceived, the precursor of the blood, which speedily begins to flow; in like manner, no sooner have bitter tidings been announced, than they pierce the soul, but the suddenness of the stroke prevents the wound from being visible at once, and the tooth of sorrow must for some space have gnawed the heart ere a vent is found for tears, which are to the mind what blood is to the body.

It was thus with me; the arrows of grief inflicted an instant wound, but their result was imperceptible until the soul had leisure to vent itself in tears and lamentations. Then, indeed, I exclaimed, "What evil genius has deluded me with this brief gleam of joy, and has shewn me my Leucippe only to lay a foundation for fresh calamities? All that has been allowed me was to see her, and I have not been permitted to satiate even the sense of sight! My pleasure has, indeed, been like the baseless fabric of a dream. O my Leucippe, how often hast thou been lost to me? Am I never to cease from tears and lamentations? Is one death perpetually to succeed another? On former occasions Fortune has been merely jesting with me, but now she is in earnest! In those former imaginary deaths of thine, some consolation, at least, was afforded me, for thy body, wholly or in part, was left at my disposal! But now thou art snatched away both in soul and body! Twice hast thou escaped the pirates, but Melitta, more foul than any pirate, has had thee done to death. And I, impious and unholy that I am, have actually kissed thy murderess, have been enfolded in her accursed embrace, and she has anticipated thee in receiving from me the offerings of Love!" While thus plunged in grief, Clinias came to visit me. I related every particular to him, and declared my determination of putting an end to my existence. He did all in his power to console me. "Consider," he said, "how often she has died and come to life again; who knows but what she may do the same on this occasion also? Why be in such haste to kill yourself? You will have abundant leisure when the tidings of her death have been positively confirmed."

"This is mere trifling," I replied; "there is small need of confirmation; my resolve is fixed, and I have decided upon a manner of death which will not permit even the hated Melitta to escape unscathed. Listen to my plan:—In case of being summoned into court it was my intention to plead not guilty. I have now changed my determination, and shall plead guilty, confessing the intrigue between Melitta and myself, and saying that we mutually planned Leucippe's death; by this means she will suffer the punishment which is her due, and I shall quit this life which I so much detest."—"Talk not thus," replied he; "can you endure to die under the base imputation of being a murderer, and, what is more, the murderer of Leucippe?"—"Nothing is base," replied I, "by which we can wreak vengeance upon our enemies." While we were engaged in argument, the fellow who had communicated the tidings of the fictitious maiden was removed, upon pretence of being taken before the magistrate to undergo an examination. Clinias and Satyrus exerted themselves, but ineffectually, in order to persuade me to alter my resolution; and on the same day they removed into lodgings, so as to be no longer under the roof of Melitta's foster-brother. The following day the case came on; Thersander had a great muster of friends and partisans, and had engaged ten advocates; and Melitta had been equally on the alert in preparing for her defence. When the counsel on either side had finished speaking, I asked leave to address the court, and said, "All those who have been exerting their eloquence, either for Thersander or for Melitta, have been giving utterance to sheer nonsense; I will reveal the whole truth, and nothing but the truth. I was once passionately in love with a female of Byzantium named Leucippe; she was carried off by pirates, and I had reason to believe that she was dead. Meeting with Melitta in Egypt, we formed a connexion, and after some time we travelled together to this city, and Leucippe, whom I just now mentioned, was found working as a slave upon Thersander's estate, under his bailiff, Sosthenes. By what means he obtained possession of a free-born female, and what were his dealings with the pirates I leave it to you to guess.

"Melitta, finding that I had recovered my former mistress, became apprehensive of her regaining her influence over my affections, and contrived a plan for putting her to death. I entered into her schemes,—

for what avails it to conceal the truth?—having received a promise that she would settle all her property upon me; a man was found, who, for the reward of a hundred gold pieces, undertook the business. When the deed was done, he fled, and is now somewhere in concealment. As for myself, Love was not long in taking vengeance upon my cruelty. No sooner did I hear of the murder being perpetrated, than I bitterly repented of what had taken place, and all my former fondness revived. For this reason I have determined to turn evidence against myself, in order that you may send me whither she is gone to whom I am still so deeply attached. Life is intolerable to one who, in addition to being a murderer, loves her of whose death he has been the cause."

Every one in court was utterly astounded at the unexpected tenour of my speech, especially Melitta. The advocates of Thersander already claimed a triumph, while those engaged in Melitta's behalf anxiously questioned her as to the truth of what I had said. She was in great confusion; denied some points, virtually admitted others, confessed to having known Leucippe, and indeed confirmed most of what I had said, with the exception of the murder. This general agreement on her part with the facts advanced by me, created a suspicion against her, even in the minds of her own counsel, and they were at a loss what line of defence to adopt on her behalf. At this critical juncture, while the court was being a scene of great clamour, Clinias came forward and requested to be heard, for "Remember," said he, "a man's life is now in jeopardy." Obtaining permission to speak, "Men of Ephesus!" he began, (his eyes filling with tears,) "do not precipitately condemn to die one who eagerly longs for death, the natural refuge of the unfortunate. He has been calumniating himself, and has taken upon him the guilt of others. Let me briefly acquaint you with what has befallen him. What he has said respecting his mistress, her being carried off by pirates, about Sosthenes, and other circumstances which happened before the pretended murder, are strictly true. The young woman has undoubtedly disappeared; but whether she is still alive, or has been made away with, it is impossible to say; one thing is certain, that Sosthenes conceived a passion for her, that he used her cruelly for not consenting to his desires, and that he was leagued with pirates. My friend believing her to be murdered, is disgusted with life, and has, therefore invented this charge against himself; he has already confessed with his own mouth that he is anxious to die owing to grief at the loss which he has sustained. Consider, I pray you, whether it is likely that one who is really a murderer would be so desirous of dying with his victim, and would feel life so insupportable. When do we ever find murderers so tender-hearted, and hatred so compassionate? In the name of the gods, therefore, do not believe his words; do not condemn to death a man who is much more deserving of commiseration than of punishment. If, as he says, he really planned this murder, let him bring forward the hired assassin; let him declare what has become of the body. If neither the one nor the other can be produced, how can any belief be attached to such a murder? 'I was in love with Melitta,' he says, 'and therefore I caused Leucippe to be killed!' How comes he to implicate Melitta, the object of his affection, and to be so desirous of dying for Leucippe, whose death he compassed? Is it usual for persons to hate the object of their love, and to love the object of their hatred? Is it not much more probable that in such circumstances he would have denied the crime (even had it been brought home to him) in order to save his mistress, instead of throwing away his own life afterwards, owing to a vain regret for her loss? What can possibly, therefore, be his motive for charging Melitta with a crime of which she is not guilty? I will tell you, and in so doing do not suppose that I have any desire of inculpating this lady,—my sole wish is to make you acquainted with the real truth.

"Before this sea-faring husband of hers came to life again so suddenly, Melitta took a violent fancy to this young man, and proposed marriage to him; he on his part was not at all disposed to comply with her wishes, and his repugnance became yet greater when he discovered that his mistress, whom he had imagined dead, was in slavery, under the power of Sosthenes. Until aware who she was, Melitta, taking pity upon her, had caused her to be set at liberty, had received her into her own house, and treated her with the consideration due to a gentlewoman in distress; but after becoming acquainted with her story, she was sent back into the country, and she has not been heard from since. The truth of what I say can be attested by Melitta herself and the two maids in whose company she was sent away. This was one thing which excited suspicions in my friend's mind that Leucippe had been foully dealt with through her rival's jealousy; a circumstance which took place after he was in prison confirmed these suspicions, and has had the effect of exasperating him not only against Melitta but against himself. One of the prisoners, in the course of lamenting his own troubles, mentioned that he had unwittingly fallen into the company of a man who had committed murder for the sake of gold; the victim was named Leucippe, and the crime, he said, had been committed at the instigation of Melitta. Of course I cannot say whether this be true or not, it is for you to institute inquiries. You can produce the prisoner who made mention of the hired assassin; Sosthenes, who can declare from whom he purchased Leucippe, and the maids, who can explain her disappearance. Before you have thoroughly investigated each of these particulars, it is contrary to all law, whether human or divine, to pass sentence upon this unfortunate young man, on the bare evidence of his frenzied words, for there can be no doubt that the violence of his grief has affected his intellect."

The arguments of Clinias appeared just and reasonable to many of those present, but Thersander's counsel, together with his friends, called out that sentence of death ought to be pronounced without delay upon the murderer who, by the providence of the gods, had been made his own accuser. Melitta brought forward her maids, and required Thersander to produce Sosthenes, who might probably turn out to be the murderer. This was the challenge mainly insisted upon by her counsel. Thersander, in great alarm, secretly despatched one of his dependants into the country, with orders to Sostratus to get out of the way at once, before the arrival of those who were about to be sent after him.

Mounting a horse without delay, the messenger rode full speed to inform the bailiff of the danger he ran of being put to the torture, if taken. Sosthenes was at that moment with Leucippe, doing his best to soothe her irritated feelings. Hearing himself summoned in a loud voice, he came out of the cottage; and, upon learning the state of matters, overcome with fear, and thinking the officers were already at his heels, he got upon the horse, and rode off towards Smyrna; after which the messenger returned to his master. It is a true saying that fear drives away the power of recollection, for Sosthenes in his alarm for his own safety was so forgetful of everything else, that he neglected to secure the door of Leucippe's cottage. Indeed slaves, generally speaking, when frightened, run into the very excess of cowardice. Melitta's advocates having given the above-mentioned challenge, Thersander came forward and said, "We have now surely had quite enough of this man's silly stories; and I cannot but feel surprised at your want of sense, who, after convicting a murderer upon the strongest possible evidence, his own admission of his guilt, do not at once pass sentence of death upon him; whereas, instead of doing this, you suffer yourselves to be imposed upon by his plausible words and tears. For my part I believe him actuated by personal fears, and to be an accomplice in the murder;

nor can I see what possible need there can be for having recourse to the rack in a matter so clear already. Nay, more, I fully believe him to have had a hand in another murder; for three days have now elapsed since I saw Sosthenes, the man whom they call upon me to bring forward; it is not at all improbable that this is owing to their contrivance, since it was he who informed me of the act of adultery which has taken place, and having put him to death, they now craftily call upon me to produce the man, knowing it to be out of my power to do so. But even supposing he were alive and present, what difference could it make? What questions would he put to him? 'Did he ever purchase a certain female?'—'Yes.' 'Was this female in the power of Melitta?'—'Yes.' Here would be an end of the examination, and Sosthenes would be dismissed. Let me now, however, address myself to Clitopho and Melitta.

"What have you done, I ask, with my slave?—for a slave of mine she assuredly was, having been purchased by Sosthenes, and were she still alive, instead of having been murdered by them, my slave she would still be." Thersander said this from mingled malice and cunning, in order that if Leucippe should turn out to be still alive, he might detain her in a state of servitude. He then continued:—"Clitopho confessed that he killed her, he has therefore pronounced judgment upon himself. Melitta, on the other hand, denies the crime—her maids may be brought forward and tortured in order to refute what she says. If it should appear that they received the young woman from her, but have not brought her back again, the question will arise, What has become of her? Why was she sent away? And to whom was she sent? Is it not self-evident that some persons had been hired to commit the murder, and that the maids were kept in ignorance of this, lest a number of witnesses might render discovery more probable? No doubt they left her at some spot where a gang of ruffians were lying in concealment, so that it was out of their power to witness what took place. He has also trumped up some story about a prisoner who made mention of the murder. I should like to know who this prisoner is, who has not said a word on the subject to the chief magistrate, but has communicated, it seems, every particular to him, except the name of his informer. Again, I ask, will you not make an end of listening to such foolery, and taking any interest in such transparent absurdities? Can you imagine that he would have turned a self-accuser without the intervention of the deity?" Thersander, after speaking to this effect, concluded by solemnly swearing that he was ignorant what had become of Sosthenes.

The presiding judge, who was of royal extraction, and who took cognizance of cases of blood, had, in accordance with the law, a certain number of assessors, men of mature age, whose province it was to assist him in judicial investigations. After conferring with them, he determined to pronounce sentence of death upon me, agreeably to a law which awarded capital punishment to any one standing convicted upon his own accusation. Melitta was to have a second trial, and her maids were to be examined by torture, Thersander was to register his oath, declaratory of his ignorance as to Sosthenes. I, as already condemned to death, was to be tortured in order to make me confess whether Melitta was privy to the murder. Already was I bound, stripped, and suspended aloft by ropes, while some were bringing scourges, others the fire and the wheel, and Clinias was lamenting loudly, and calling upon the gods, when lo! the priest of Diana crowned with laurel, was beheld approaching: the sign of a sacred embassy coming to offer sacrifices to the goddess. In such cases there is suspension of all judicial punishments during the days occupied in the performance of the sacrifice, and in consequence of this I was released. The chief of the sacred embassy was no other than Leucippe's father. Diana had appeared to the Byzantians, and had secured them victory in the war against the Thracians, in consequence of which they felt bound to send her a sacrifice in token of their gratitude. In addition to this, the goddess had appeared to Sostratus himself at night, signifying to him that he would find his daughter and his nephew at Ephesus. Just about this time, Leucippe perceived the door of the cottage to be left open; and as, after a careful examination, Sosthenes was nowhere to be seen, her usual presence of mind and sanguine hopes returned. She remembered how often, contrary to all expectation, she had been preserved, and the thought of this gave her increased boldness. Fortune moreover favoured her, since the temple of Diana was near the spot. Accordingly, hurrying thither, she sought refuge within its precincts. The temple afforded sanctuary to men and virgins,—any other woman incurred death by entering it, unless she happened to be a slave who had some cause of complaint against her master; in which case she was permitted to take refuge there, and the matter was submitted to the decision of the magistrates; supposing the master was acquitted, he took back his slave, being bound by oath to bear her no ill will on account of her having run away; but if, on the contrary, the slave was proved to have justice on her side, she remained in the temple, and was employed in the service of the goddess. Leucippe arrived at the temple just at the time when Sostratus was conducting the priest to the scene of the trial, in order to suspend the proceedings, and was very near encountering her father.

When I was set free, the court broke up, and I was surrounded by a concourse of people, some pitying me, some calling upon the gods in my behalf, others questioning me. Sostratus, coming by at the time, no sooner saw than he recognized me; for, as I before mentioned, he had formerly been at Tyre upon the occasion of a festival of Hercules, and had passed a considerable time there before the period of our flight. He at once knew me, and the more readily because his dream had led him to expect that he should find me and his daughter there. Coming up to me, therefore, "Do I see Clitopho?" said he; "and where is Leucippe?" Instantly recognizing him, I cast my eyes to the ground and remained silent, while the bystanders related to him every particular relative to my self-accusation. He no sooner heard what they had to say than with an exclamation of bitter grief, and smiting his head he made a rush at me, and was very near pulling out my eyes, for I remained altogether passive and offered no resistance to his violence. At length Clinias coming forward, checked his fury, and endeavoured to pacify him. "What are you about?" said he: "why are you venting your wrath against him; he loves Leucippe more dearly than you do, for he has courted death from belief that she was no longer in existence;" and he added a great deal more in order to calm his irritation. He, on the other hand, continued to vent his grief, and to call upon Diana. "Is it for this that thou hast summoned me hither, O goddess? Is this the fulfilment of my vision? I gave credence to the dreams which thou didst send, and flattered myself that I should find my daughter! In lieu of which thou offerest me, forsooth, a welcome present,—my daughter's murderer!" Hearing of the vision sent by Diana, Clinias was overjoyed. "Take courage, sir," he said; "the goddess will not belie herself! Rest assured your daughter is alive; believe me, I am prophesying truth; do you not remark how wonderfully she has rescued your nephew from the clutches of his torturers?"

While this was going on, one of the ministers of the goddess came hurriedly to the priest, and announced that a foreign maiden had taken refuge in the temple. This intelligence, given in my hearing, inspired me with new life; my hopes revived, and I summoned courage to look up. "My prediction is being fulfilled, sir," said Clinias, addressing Sostratus; and then turning to the messenger he inquired, "Is the maiden handsome?"— "She is second in beauty only to Diana herself," was the reply.

At these words I leaped for joy, and exclaimed, "It must be Leucippe!"—"You are right in your conjecture," said he; "this was the very name she gave; saying likewise that she was the daughter of one Sostratus, and a native of Byzantium." Clinias now clapped his hands and shouted with delight, while Sostratus, overcome by his emotions, was ready to sink upon the ground. For my part, in spite of my fetters, I made a bound into the air, and then shot away towards the temple, like an arrow from a bow. The keepers pursued me, supposing that I was trying to escape, and bawled out to every one "Stop him! stop him!" At that moment, however, I seemed to have wings upon my heels, and it was with much difficulty that some persons at length caught hold of me in my mad career. The keepers upon coming up were disposed to use violence, to which, however, I was no longer inclined to submit; nevertheless they persisted in dragging me towards the prison. By this time Clinias and Sostratus had arrived at the spot; and the former called out, "Whither are you taking this man?—he is not guilty of the murder for which he has been condemned!" Sostratus spoke to the same effect, and added that he was father to the maiden supposed to have been murdered. The bystanders, learning the circumstances which had taken place, were loud in their praises of Diana, and surrounding me would not permit me to be taken to prison; on the other hand, the keepers declared that they had no authority to set a prisoner at liberty who had been condemned to death. In the end, the priest, at the urgent entreaty of Sostratus, agreed to become bail, and to produce me in court whenever it should be required. Then at length freed from my fetters, I hurried on towards the temple, followed by Sostratus, whose feelings of joy could hardly, I think, equal my own.

Rumour, who outstrips the swiftest of men, had already reached Leucippe, and informed her of all particulars respecting me and Sostratus. Upon catching sight of us she darted out of the temple, and threw her arms around her father, but at the same time her looks were turned on me; the presence of Sostratus restrained me from embracing her, though I gazed intently upon her face; and thus our greetings were confined to eyes.

Book VIII

Just as we were sitting down and beginning to converse upon the various events which had taken place, Thersander, accompanied by several witnesses, arrived in a great bustle, and addressing himself to the priest in a loud voice said, "I warn you, in the presence of these witnesses, that you have acted illegally in setting at liberty a prisoner condemned to death; besides which, what right have you to detain my slave, a lewd woman, who is insatiable in her appetite for men?" Exasperated by this language, and not enduring to hear her called a slave and accused of lewdness, I interrupted him, "You are trebly a slave yourself, and the rankest lecher who ever existed, where as she is free born, and pure and worthy of her guardian goddess!"—"Dare you vent your insolence on me, convicted felon that you are?" exclaimed he, accompanying his words with a couple of blows, which, given with all his might, caused the blood to flow from my nose in streams; in his haste to deal me a third, he struck me on the mouth, and my teeth inflicting a severe wound upon his fingers avenged the insult offered to my nostrils. Uttering a cry of pain, he drew back his hand, and did not offer any further violence; while, pretending not to notice that he was hurt, I filled the temple with outcries at the usage which I had received. "Whither," I exclaimed, "shall we henceforth flee to escape the hands of violence? Where shall we seek sanctuary, if Diana is despised? Lo! I have been attacked in the very temple, and struck in front of the holy curtain! I had supposed that such acts could take place only in some howling wilderness, with no human witness to behold them; but you—abandoned wretch that you are!—exercise your brutality in the very presence of the gods! Temples are wont to afford an asylum, even to the guilty; but I, who am wholly innocent and a suppliant of the goddess, have suffered violence before the altar,—nay, before the eyes of the goddess! The blows inflicted on me have virtually fallen upon Diana herself! Nor has your drunken fury been content with blows, you have even dealt wounds, such as one receives in battle, and you have defiled the sacred pavement with human blood! Who ever poured out such drink offerings to the Ephesian goddess? Barbarians do so, and so do the Tauri, and blood is sprinkled upon the altars of the Scythian Diana; but you have made a savage Scythia of the polished Ionia, and the gore fit only for Tauris is seen to flow at Ephesus! Why not proceed yet farther, and draw your sword against me?

Though what need is there of swords, the work of a weapon has already been accomplished by your naked hand! Yes! your blood-stained and homicidal hand has done deeds fit only for a scene of murder!"

Attracted by my outcries, a crowd of those who were in the temple flocked together, who rated him soundly for his conduct, and the priest himself said, "Are you not ashamed to exhibit such behaviour openly and in the temple?" Encouraged by their presence, "Men of Ephesus!" I said, "you see how foully I have been treated. Yes! I, a free man and a native of no mean city, have had a plot contrived against my life by this wicked man, and have been preserved only by the intervention of Diana, who has brought to light the falsehood of the charge against me. It behoves me now to go forth in order to cleanse my face; I may not do so within the temple, lest the holy water should be defiled by the blood of violence." Thersander was with difficulty forced out, and muttered to himself as he departed: "Your fate is already sealed, and ere long the law shall have its due; as for this strumpet who would fain pass for a virgin, she shall undergo the ordeal of the syrinx." When at last we were rid of him, I went out and cleansed my face; it was now supper-time, and the priest entertained us very hospitably.

I could not summon up courage to look Sostratus in the face, from a recollection of what had been my conduct towards him, and he perceiving this, and guessing my feelings, was equally unwilling to look towards me; Leucippe also sat with downcast eyes, so that the supper was altogether a very solemn affair. When however the wine circulated, and reserve began to disappear under the influence of Bacchus, patron of freedom and ease, the priest, addressing Sostratus, said, "My worthy guest, will you not favour us with your own history?—it must, I imagine, contain some interesting passages, and the listening to such subjects adds zest to the wine." Sostratus readily availed himself of the opportunity to speak, and replied, "My own story is a very simple one; you are already acquainted with my name and country, and when I have added that I am uncle to this young man and father to the maiden, you have heard all.—Do you, son Clitopho, (turning to me) lay aside all bashfulness and relate whatever you have to say worth hearing; the grief and vexation which I have endured is to be attributed to Fortune not to you; besides, to tell of past troubles when one has escaped from them, is a source of pleasure rather than of grief."

Upon this, I detailed all the events which had occurred since leaving Tyre—the voyage, the shipwreck, our being cast upon the coast of

Egypt, our falling among the buccaneers, the carrying off of Leucippe, the adventures of the false stomach contrived by Menelaus, the passion conceived for her by the commander, the discovery of the love potion by Chæreas, Leucippe's second rape by corsairs, and the wound received by me of which I exhibited the scar. When I approached the subject of Melitta, I related the story in such a manner as to give an exalted idea of my own continence, yet without being guilty of any falsehood. I spoke of her violent passion for me, her urgent but unsuccessful entreaties to obtain its gratification, her munificent promises, her grief at being disappointed, our subsequent voyage to Ephesus, the supper, my sharing her bed, and (invoking at the same time Diana's name) my rising from her side as pure as one female would from another, my being seized and put in prison, my false accusation of myself; this and every other matter I detailed down to the appearance of the Sacred Embassy, suppressing only the disgrace of my connexion with Melitta.

"Leucippe's adventures," said I, in continuation, "are stranger even than mine. She has been sold to slavery, has been compelled to labour in the field, has been despoiled of the honours of her head, of which you can see the tokens;" and then passing on to the conduct of Sosthenes and Thersander, I entered much more into detail than I had done, when speaking of myself. My object in doing this, was to gratify Leucippe, in the hearing of her father. "She has endured every ill in her person," said I, "excepting one, and to avoid that one, she has submitted to all the others; and has continued, to this day, father (addressing Sostratus), pure as when first you sent her from Byzantium. It is no merit in me to have abstained from consummating the object for which we fled; the merit is entirely on her side for having preserved inviolate her chastity in the midst of villains, nay, against that arch villain, the shameless and violent Thersander. Our flight from home was caused by mutual love; but I can assure you, father, that during the voyage we were quite platonic, our intercourse was no other than that of a brother and a sister; and if there be such a thing as virginity in men, I am still a virgin as regards Leucippe; she, long since bound herself by a vow to Diana.

"Queen of love," exclaimed I, "be not wroth nor deem thyself to have been slighted by us! we were but unwilling to celebrate our nuptials in the absence of the maiden's father; he has now happily arrived; be thou present therefore, and smile propitiously upon us." The priest had listened open-mouthed to my story, and Sostratus had been shedding tears during the recital of his daughter's sufferings. "Now that you have heard the account of our adventures," said I to our host, "I have a favour to ask of you. What did Thersander's parting words refer to, when he made mention of the syrinx?"—"You have a right to make the inquiry," replied he; "and I am both able and willing to comply with your request. It will be some return for the narrative with which you have just favoured us. You see the grove in the rear of the temple; in it is a cave, entrance into which is forbidden to women in general, but is permitted to maidens who have preserved their purity. A little within the doors a syrinx is suspended; perhaps you Byzantians are already acquainted with the nature of this instrument; should it be otherwise, I will give you a description of it, and will likewise relate the legend of Pan, with which it is connected.

"The syrinx is composed of a certain number of reed pipes, which collectively produce the same sounds as a flute; these reeds are placed in regular order and mutually compacted, presenting the same appearance on either side; beginning from the shortest, they ascend in gradation to the longest, and the central one holds a medium proportion between the two extremities. The principle of this arrangement arises from the laws of harmony, the two extremes of sound (as well as of length) are found at either end, and the intervening pipes convey downwards a gradation of notes so as to combine the first and shrillest with the last and deepest of all. The same variety of sounds, (as before observed) are produced by Minerva's flute as by the syrinx of Pan; but in the former case, the fingers direct the notes, in the latter, the mouth supplies the place; in the one case, the performer closes every opening except the one through which the breath is intended to proceed; in the other case, he leaves open the aperture of every other reed, and places his mouth upon that one only which he wishes to emit a sound; his lips leap (as we may say) from reed to reed and dance along the syrinx; as the laws of harmony require. Now, this syrinx was originally neither pipe nor reed, but a damsel whose charms made her most desirable. Smitten by love, Pan pursued her, and she fled for refuge to a thicket; the god still closely following her, stretched forth his hand to seize as he supposed her hair, but lo! instead of hair, he grasped a bunch of reeds, which, so the legend says, sprang from the earth as she descended into it. Enraged at his disappointment, Pan cut them down, imagining that they had stolen from him the object of his love; but when his search after her still proved unavailing, he supposed the maiden to have been changed into these reeds, and wept at his hasty act, thinking that in so doing he had caused the death of his beloved. He then proceeded to collect and place together what he imagined to be her limbs, and holding them in his hands, continued to kiss what fancy pictured to be the mangled remains of the maiden's body. Deeply sighing as he imprinted kisses on the reeds, his sighs found a passage through these hollow pipes, forming sounds of music, and thus the syrinx came to have a voice. This instrument Pan suspended within the cave, and he is said often to resort hither in order to play upon it. At a period subsequent to the event of which I am speaking, he conveyed the place as a gift to Diana, upon the condition that none save a spotless maiden should be allowed to enter it. Whenever therefore the virginity of any female comes into suspicion, she is conducted to the entrance of this cavern, and it is left to the syrinx to pronounce judgment upon her. She enters in her usual dress, and immediately the doors are closed. If she proves to be a virgin, a sweetly clear and divinely ravishing sound is heard, caused either by the air which is there stored up, finding its way into the syrinx, or by the lips of the god himself. After a short space, the doors open of their own accord, and the maiden makes her appearance, wearing a crown of pine leaves. If, on the other hand, the female has falsely asserted her claim to virginity, the syrinx is silent, and instead of music, the cave sends forth a doleful sound, upon which those who attended her to the entrance depart and leave her to her fate. Three days after, the priestess of the temple enters, and finds the syrinx fallen to the ground, but the female is no where to be seen. I have now told you everything, and it is for you maturely to deliberate upon what course you intend pursuing. If, as I sincerely hope, the maiden is a virgin, you may fearlessly submit to the ordeal, for the syrinx has never falsified its character. Should the case be otherwise, it is needless to suggest what is the safer course; and you well know, what a female, exposed as she has been to various perils, may have been compelled to submit to, quite against her will."

Eagerly interrupting the priest, Leucippe said, "You need be under no alarm on my account, I am quite ready to enter, and be shut up within the cave."—"I rejoice to hear you say so," replied he, "and I congratulate you on the good fortune which has preserved your virtue." As it was near evening we retired to the chambers prepared for us by the priest; Clinias had not supped with us from fear of being burdensome to our kind host, but had returned to his former lodgings. The legend of the syrinx caused Sostratus much uneasiness, as he evidently feared, that out of regard to him, we had been advancing undue claims to chastity; perceiving this, I made a sign to Leucippe to remove as best she could, the suspicions of her father. His anxiety had not escaped her observation, and even before receiving a hint from me, she had been devising how to set his mind at rest. Upon embracing him, therefore, as he retired to rest, "Father," she said, in a low voice, "you need be under no apprehension; I solemnly swear to you by Diana, that both of us have spoken nothing but the truth." The following day, Sostratus and the priest were occupied in performing the object of the sacred embassy, by offering the victims; the members of the Senate were present at the solemnity, and hymns of praise resounded in honour of the goddess. Thersander also was there, and coming to the president he desired to have his case postponed to the next day, as the condemned criminal had been set at liberty by some meddling persons, and Sosthenes could no where be found. His request was complied with, and we on our part, made every preparation for meeting the charge which was to be brought against us. When the morning of trial arrived, Thersander spoke as follows:—"I am utterly at a loss how to begin, and against whom first to direct my charges; the offence which has given rise to this trial involves various others equal in importance, and implicates several parties, and each of their offences might supply matter for a separate trial; my words must almost unavoidably fail in doing justice to each division of the subject, and in my eagerness to hasten to some point hitherto untouched, I must necessarily deal imperfectly with that upon which I am engaged. How indeed can it be otherwise in a case like this, wherein is mixed up adultery, impiety, bloodshed and lawless excesses of every kind! Where adulterers are found murdering other people's slaves, murderers corrupting other people's wives, whoremongers and harlots interrupting and disgracing with their presence holy solemnities and the most sacred places? Nevertheless I will proceed. You condemned a criminal to death—on account of what cause, it matters not—you sent him back in chains to prison, there to be kept until the execution of the sentence; yet this man who is virtually your prisoner, now stands before you at liberty and attired in white; aye, and no doubt will venture to raise his voice in order to declaim against me—or rather, I should say, against you and against the justice of your verdict. I demand to have the sentence of the Court read aloud.—There, you have now heard it. 'The sentence of the Court is that Clitopho be put to death.'—Where then is the executioner? Let the prisoner be led away, let the hemlock be administered—he is already dead in law, and has lived a day too long. And now, what excuse have you to plead, holy and reverend priest?

In which of the sacred laws do you find it laid down that prisoners, duly condemned by a sentence of the court, and delivered up to chains and death, are to be rescued and set at liberty? On what grounds do you arrogate to yourself a power superior to that of the judges and the Court? President! it is time for you to quit your chair and to abdicate to him your place and power! Your authority is gone, your decrees are good for nought! He takes upon himself to reverse the sentence you have passed.—Why any longer stand among us, sir Priest, as a mere private individual? By all means go up higher, take your place upon the bench; issue henceforth your judgments, or if it please you better, your arbitrary and tyrannical decrees; spurn law and justice under your feet; believe that you are more than man; claim for yourself worship next after Diana, since you have already arrogated her peculiar privilege. Hitherto she alone has afforded sanctuary to suppliants, but to suppliants, be it remembered, whom the law has not yet condemned;—not those to whom chains and death have been decreed, for the altar should be a refuge not to the wicked but to the unfortunate! You, forsooth, liberate a prisoner; you acquit a condemned criminal! You therefore arrogate a power superior to that of Diana's self! Who, until now, ever heard of a murderer and adulterer inhabiting the chamber of a temple, instead of the dungeon of a prison? A foul adulterer under the same roof with a virgin goddess, and having for his partner a shameless woman, a slave and runaway! You it is who have entertained the worthy pair at bed and board; nay, probably have shared her bed. You have converted the temple of the goddess into a common brothel. You have made her sanctuary, a den of whoremongers and harlots; your doings would hardly find a parallel in the vilest stew! So far as regards these two I have now done, one will I trust meet with his just deserts, let the sentence of the law be put in force against the other.

"My second charge is against Melitta for adultery; and here I need not speak at any length, as it has already been decided that her maids shall be submitted to the torture, in order to ascertain the truth. I demand, therefore, to have them produced; and if, after undergoing the question, they persist in denying their knowledge that the accused has for a considerable time cohabited with her in my house, not only in the character of paramour but of husband, then I am bound freely to acquit her of all blame. But should the contrary be proved, then I claim that in accordance with the laws she be deprived of her marriage portion, and that it be given up to me, in which case the prisoner must suffer death, the punishment awarded to adulterers. Whether, however, he shall suffer under this charge or as a murderer, matters little; he is guilty of both crimes, and though suffering punishment will, in fact, be evading justice,—for whereas he owes two deaths, he will have paid but one. One other subject there remains for me to touch upon: this slave of mine and her respectable pretended father. I shall, however, reserve what I have to say on this head until you have come to a decision respecting the other parties."

Thersander having now ended, it was for the priest to speak. He was possessed of eloquence, and had in him a large share of the Aristophanic vein; accordingly he attacked Thersander's debauched manner of life with great wit and humour. "By the goddess," said he, "it is the sign of having a foul tongue, thus shamelessly to rail against honest folks,— but it is nothing new to this worthy gentleman, for throughout his life the filthiness of his tongue has been notorious. The season of his youth was passed among the lewdest of mankind, among whom he gave himself up to the most abandoned practices, and while affecting gravity, sobriety, and a regard for learning, his body was made the slave of all impurity. After a time he left his father's house, and hired a miserable lodging, where he took up his abode. And how do you suppose he earned his living? Why, partly by strolling about the town and singing ballads, partly by receiving at home fellows like himself, for purposes which I shall not now name. All this time he was supposed to be cultivating his mind, and improving his education; whereas, accomplished hypocrite! he was but throwing a veil over his iniquities. Even in the wrestling school his manner while anointing his body, and his attitudes, and his always choosing to engage in wrestling with the stoutest and comeliest of the youths, showed his detestable propensities. Such was his character during his youthful days. Upon arriving at manhood, he threw off the mask, and exhibited before the eyes of all the vices which hitherto he had endeavoured to keep concealed.

"As he could no longer turn any other part of his body to account, he determined thenceforth to exercise his tongue, and admirably has he succeeded in sharpening it upon the whetstone of impurity, making his mouth the vehicle for shameless speech, pouring out its torrents of abuse on every one, and having his effrontery stamped upon his very face, he has gone the length (as you have seen) of coarsely insulting in your presence an individual whom you have honoured with the priesthood. Were I a stranger to you, and had not my life been passed among you, I should deem it necessary to dwell upon my own character, and that of my usual associates; but there is no occasion for doing this. You well know how opposite has been my way of living to the slanderous imputations which he has cast upon me. I therefore pass on at once to his recent charges. I have set at liberty, he says, a convicted criminal; and upon these grounds he proceeds to inveigh bitterly against me, and applies to me the epithet of tyrant, and I know not how many other hard words. Now a tyrant is one who oppresses the innocent, not one who steps forward to defend the victim of false accusation. What law, I demand, sanctioned your committing this young man to prison? Before what tribunal had he been condemned? What judge had pronounced his sentence? Granting the truth of every charge advanced against him, he has at all events a right to a fair trial; he has a right to be heard in his own defence; he has a right to be legally convicted! If need be, let the law (which is supreme over all alike,) imprison him; until it has altered its decrees not one of us can claim authority over another. But if proceedings such as we have seen, are to be countenanced, it would be advisable at once to close the courts, to abolish the tribunals, to depose the magistrates. With far greater justice may I retort against him the expressions which he has employed respecting me. I may say, President, make way for Thersander, for your presidentship is but an empty name,—it is he who really exercises your powers; nay, more, exercises powers which you do not possess. You have assessors, without whose concurrence you can pass no sentence. You can exercise no authority except upon the judgment seat; you cannot sit at home and condemn a man to chains and prisons. This worshipful gentleman, however, is both judge and jury; all offices are, forsooth, concentrated in his single person; he makes his house his court of justice; there he inflicts his punishments; thence he issues his decrees and condemns a man to chains; and to make matters yet better, he holds his court at night! And what is it which now finds employment for his lungs? 'You have set free,' he says, 'a criminal condemned to death.' I ask, What death? I ask, What criminal?—for what crime condemned? 'For murder,' he replies. A murderer! Where, then, is the murdered victim? She whom you declared to have been done to death, stands before you alive and well. The charge, therefore, at once falls to the ground, for you cannot consider this maiden as an airy phantom, sent up by Pluto from the realms below! You are yourself a murderer,—aye, and a double murderer. Her you have slain by lying words; him you wished in reality to slay.

I may add her also; for we know of your doings in the country. The great goddess Diana has, however, happily preserved them both, by delivering the maiden from the hands of Sosthenes, and this young man from you. As for Sosthenes, you have purposely got him out of the way, in order to escape detection. Are you not ashamed to have your charges against these strangers proved to be the vilest calumnies? What I have said will have sufficed to clear myself; the defence of the strangers I shall leave to others."

An advocate of considerable reputation as an orator, and a member of the senate, was about to address the court on behalf of me and Melitta, when he was interrupted by one of Thersander's counsel, named Sopater:—"Brother Nicostralus," said he, "I must claim the right of being first heard against this adulterous couple; it will be your turn to reply afterwards.

"What Thersander said related only to the priest, and scarcely touched upon the case of the prisoner; and when I shall prove him to be richly deserving of a two-fold death, then will be the time for you to rebut my charges." Then, stroking his chin, and with a great flourish of words, he proceeded:—"We have listened to the buffoonery of this priest, venting his scurrilous falsehoods against Thersander, and endeavouring to turn against him the language so justly directed against himself. Now, I maintain, that throughout Thersander has adhered to truth; the priest has taken upon himself to liberate a prisoner; he has received a harlot beneath his roof; he has been on friendly terms with an adulterer. Not a word has he uttered against Thersander but what savours of the vilest calumny, but if anything especially becomes a priest, surely it is to keep a civil tongue in his head,—and in saying this I am but borrowing his own words. However, after edifying us with his wit and jests, he went on to adopt a tragic strain, and bitterly inveighed against us for handcuffing an adulterer, and sending him to prison. I wonder what it cost to kindle in him this prodigious warmth of zeal? Methinks I can give a tolerably shrewd guess. He has looked with a longing eye upon the features of these two shameless guests of his; the wench is handsome, the youth has a goodly countenance; both are well suited for the private pleasures of a priest! Which of the two best served your turn? At any rate you all slept together; you all got drunk together; and there are no witnesses to depose how your nights were passed. I sadly fear me that Diana's fane has been perverted into Aphrodite's temple! It will furnish matter for future discussion whether you are fit to be a priest. As to my client

Thersander, every one knows that from his earliest years he has been a pattern of sobriety and virtue; no sooner was he arrived at manhood, than he contracted a marriage according to the laws; his choice was indeed unfortunate, and trusting to her rank and wealth, he found himself the husband of a wife very different from what he had expected. There can be little doubt that she long ago went astray, unknown to this most exemplary of men; it is plain enough that latterly she has cast off all shame, and has indulged her disgraceful propensities to the utmost. No sooner had her husband set out on a long voyage than she thought it a favourable opportunity for indulging her loose desires; and then it was that, unfortunately for her, she lighted upon this 'masculine whore;' a paramour who among women is a man, and among men a woman.

"Not content to cohabit with him in impunity in a foreign land, she must needs transport him with her over an extent of sea, and on the voyage must needs take her lascivious sport in the sight of all the passengers. O, shameless adultery, in which sea and land, had both a share. O shameless adultery, prolonged even from Egypt to Ionia! Generally, when women are guilty of adultery they confine themselves to a single act, or if they repeat their crime, it is with every precaution which may ensure concealment. In the present case, however, she commits the sin by sound of trumpet, if I may so say. The adulterer is known to every one in Ephesus, and she herself is not ashamed to have brought him hither like so much merchandise; making an investment in good looks, taking in a paramour by way of freight! She will say, 'I concluded my husband to be dead.' 'In that case,' I reply, 'were your husband dead, you would be free from criminality, for there would then be no sufferer by the adulterous act, nor is any dishonour cast on marriage if the husband is no longer in existence; but if the husband be alive, the marriage bond is still in force, his rights over his wife continue, and he has, by her criminality, suffered a grievous wrong.'"

Thersander here interrupted him, "It is needless to examine any one by torture, as was formerly proposed. I offer two challenges: one to this wife of mine, Melitta; the other to the pretended daughter of this ambassador, who is lawfully my slave." He then read aloud; "I Thersander challenge Melitta and Leucippe (such I understand is the strumpet's name) to submit to the following ordeal:—If the former, as she asserts, has had no intercourse with this stranger during the period of my absence, let her go unto the sacred fountain of the Styx, declare her innocence upon oath, and then stand acquitted of any further guilt.

Let the latter, if free-born and no longer a maiden, remain my slave, for the temple of the goddess affords sanctuary to slaves alone; if, on the other hand, she asserts herself to be a virgin, let her be shut into the cave of the syrinx." We immediately accepted this challenge, being already aware that it would be made.

Melitta, likewise conscious that nothing improper had taken place during the actual absence of Thersander, said, "I accept the challenge; and will here add, that during the period referred to I had criminal intercourse with no one, whether foreigner or citizen; and I will ask you," addressing Thersander, "to what penalty will you submit, provided the charge prove groundless and calumnious?"—"I will submit to whatever the law decrees," was his reply. The court then broke up, the following day being appointed for the respective ordeals referred to in the challenge. The following is the legend of the Stygian fountain:—

"There was once a beauteous maiden, named Rhodopis, whose supreme delight was in the chase. She was swift of foot, unerring in her aim; she wore a head-band, had her robe girt up to the knee, and her hair short, after the fashion of men. Diana met her, bestowed many commendations on her, and made her her companion in the chase. The maiden bound herself by oath to observe perpetual virginity, to avoid the company of men, and never to humiliate herself by submitting to amorous indulgence. Venus overheard the oath, and was incensed at it, and determined to punish the damsel for her presumption. There happened to be a youth of Ephesus, named Euthynicus, as much distinguished among men for beauty as Rhodopis was among those of her own sex. He was as ardently devoted to the chase as the maiden, and like her was averse to the delights of love. One day when Diana was absent, Venus contrived to make the game which they were following run in the same direction; then addressing her archer son, she said, 'Do you see yon frigid and unloving pair, enemies to us and to our mysteries? The maiden has even gone the length of registering an oath against me! Do you see them both following a hind? Join the chase, and begin by making an example of the maiden;—your arrows never miss.' Both at the same moment bend their bows,—she against the hind, but Cupid against her,—and both hit the mark, but the successful huntress herself becomes a victim; her arrow pierces the shoulder of the deer, but Cupid's shaft penetrates her heart, and the result of the wound was love for Euthynicus. Cupid then aims a shaft at him, and with the same effect. For a time they stand and gaze upon each other;

their eyes are fascinated; they cannot turn away; gradually their inward wounds become inflamed; the fire kindles, and love urges their steps to the cavern where now the fountain flows, and there they violate their oath. Diana soon after saw Venus laughing, and readily comprehended what had taken place, and as a punishment changed the maiden into a fountain, upon the spot where her chastity was lost. For this reason, when any female is suspected of impurity, she is made to step into the fountain, which is shallow, reaching only to midleg, and then it is that the ordeal takes place. The oath declarative of chastity is written on a tablet, and suspended from her neck; if truly sworn, the fountain remains unmoved; if falsely taken, it swells and rages, rises to her neck, and flows over the tablet."

Next morning a great concourse assembled, and at the head came Thersander, with a confident expression of countenance, and looking at us with a contemptuous smile. Leucippe was attired in a sacred robe of fine white linen, reaching to the feet and girded about her waist; round her head she had a purple fillet, and her feet were bare. She entered the cavern with an air of becoming modesty. Upon seeing her disappear within, I was overcome by agitation, and said mentally, "I doubt not your chastity, dearest Leucippe, but I am afraid of Pan; he is a virgin-loving god, and for aught I know, you may become a second syrinx. His former mistress easily escaped him, for her course lay over an open plain; whereas you are shut up within doors, and so blockaded that flight is out of the question, however much you may wish to fly. O Pan! be thou propitious; do not violate the statutes of the place, which we have religiously observed; grant that Leucippe may again return to us a virgin; remember thy compact with Diana, and do no injury to the maiden." While talking to myself in this manner, sounds of music proceeded from the cavern, more ravishingly sweet, I was assured, than had been heard on any former occasion: the doors were immediately opened, and when Leucippe sprang forth, the multitude shouted with delight, and vented execrations upon Thersander. What my own feelings were, I cannot pretend to describe. After gaining this first signal triumph, we left the spot, and proceeded to the place which was to be the scene of the remaining ordeal, the people following again to behold the spectacle. Everything was in readiness, the tablet was suspended to Melitta's neck, and she descended into the shallow fountain with a smiling countenance. No change was perceptible in the water, which remained perfectly still, and did not in the slightest degree exceed its usual depth, and at the expiration of the allotted time the president came forward, and taking Melitta by the hand, conducted her out of the fountain. Thersander, already twice defeated, and surely anticipating a third defeat, took to his heels and fled to his own house, fearing that the people would, in their fury, stone him. His apprehensions were well founded, for some young men were seen at a distance dragging Sosthenes along; two of them were Melitta's kinsmen, and the others were servants, whom she had despatched in quest of him. Thersander had caught sight of him, and feeling sure that when put to the torture he would confess everything, he secretly left the city, as soon as night came on. Sosthenes was committed to prison by order of the magistrates, and we returned triumphant upon every point, and accompanied by the shouts and good wishes of the people.

Next morning they whose business it was conducted Sosthenes before the magistrates. Aware that he was about to be put to the question, he made a full confession of everything, stating how far Thersander had been the prime agent, and how far he had himself assisted in carrying out his schemes! nor did he omit to repeat the conversation which had taken place between his master and him before the cottage-door. He was sent back to prison there to await his sentence, and a decree of banishment was pronounced against Thersander. When this business was concluded, we again returned to the hospitable dwelling of the priest, and while at supper resumed the subject of our former conversation, mutually relating any incidents which had previously been omitted. Leucippe, now that the purity of her character was fully established, no longer stood in awe of her father, but took pleasure in narrating the events which had befallen her. When she came to that part of her story which referred to Pharos and the pirates, I requested her to give us every particular about them, and especially to explain the riddle of the severed head, as this alone was wanting to complete the history of her adventures. "The recital will interest us all," I said, "especially your father."

"The unhappy female to whom you allude," replied Leucippe, "was one of that class who sell their charms for money. She was inveigled on board, under pretence of becoming the wife of a sea captain, and remained there in ignorance of the real cause for which she had been brought, passing her time in the company of one of the pirates, who pretended to have a passion for her. When I was seized, they placed me, as you saw, in a boat, and rowed off with all their might; and afterwards when they perceived that the vessel despatched in pursuit was gaining upon them, they stripped the wretched woman of her clothes, which they put on me, making her dress herself in mine; then placing her at the stern in sight of the pursuers, they cut off her head and cast the body overboard, doing the same with the head, when the pursuit was given up. Whether she had been brought on board for the above purpose, or in order to be sold, as they afterwards told me, I cannot say; certain it is that she was put to death by way of eluding the pursuers, the pirates imagining that I should fetch more money as a slave than she would do. It was this determination on their part which earned his just reward for Chæreas, who had suggested the murder of the female in place of me. The pirates refused to let him retain exclusive possession of me, saying that on his account one woman had already been lost to them, who would have been a source of gain. They proposed, therefore, that I should be sold to make up the loss, and that the money should be equally divided. He replied in an angry and threatening manner, asserting his prior claims, and reminding them of their compact, and that I had been carried off, not in order to be sold, but to be his mistress. Upon this, one of the pirates came behind him, and dealt him his measure of justice by striking off his head and flinging his body into the sea,—a worthy requital of his perfidious conduct towards me.

"After two days' sail, the pirates put in at some place, the name of which I do not know, where they sold me to a merchant who used to traffic with them, and from his hands I passed into the possession of Sosthenes."

"My children," said Sostratus, when Leucippe had concluded, "I will now relate what has happened to Calligone, for it is but fair that I should contribute my share to the conversation." Upon hearing my sister's name mentioned, I became all attention, and said, "Prithee, sir, proceed; I shall rejoice to hear that she is still alive." He commenced by repeating what has already been mentioned respecting Callisthenes, the oracle given to the Byzantians, the sacred embassy sent to Tyre, and the stratagem for carrying off Calligone. He went on to say: "Callisthenes discovered during the voyage that she was not my daughter; but although matters had thus turned out quite contrary to his intentions, he conceived a strong passion for his fair captive, and throwing himself at her knees: 'Lady,' he said, 'do not imagine that I am a corsair or a villain; I am of good birth, and second in rank to none in Byzantium. It is Love who has compelled me to turn pirate, and to employ this stratagem against you. Deign, therefore, to consider me your slave from this day forth. I offer you my hand in marriage. You shall have for your dowry more wealth than your father would have bestowed upon you, and you shall preserve your maiden state so long as you may please.'

"By means of these, and other insinuating words, he brought her to look favourably upon him, for he was handsome in person and possessed a flow of persuasive language. Upon arriving at Byzantium he had a deed drawn up assigning her an ample dowry; he then proceeded to make other preparations, purchased for her splendid dresses, jewellery and ornaments, in short, whatsoever was required for the wardrobe and toilette of a lady of rank and wealth. Having done this, he abstained from soliciting her virtue, and in fulfilment of his promise allowed her to remain a maiden, and thus he gradually won her affections. In a short time, quite a wonderful alteration took place in the young man; he became conciliatory in manner, and prudent and orderly in his mode of living; he shewed respect by rising up before his elders, and was the first courteously to salute any whom he met; his former indiscriminate profusion, which had been mere lavish prodigality, now became wisely directed liberality, choosing for its objects those who were suffering from poverty and required assistance.

"All who remembered his former and dissolute course of life were amazed at this sudden change. He shewed me the most marked attention, and I could not help loving him and attributing his former conduct more to an excess of open-heartedness than to any actual vicious propensities, and I called to mind the case of Themistocles, who after a youth spent in licentiousness, in after life excelled all his countrymen in soundness of judgment and many virtues. I really felt sorry at having repulsed him, when he was a suitor for my daughter's hand, he treated me with so much respect, giving me the title of father, and escorting me whenever I had occasion to go through the forum. He likewise took great interest in military exercises, especially in what related to the cavalry department; he had always been fond of horses, but hitherto merely to indulge his love of amusement and his luxurious tastes; yet though actuated by no higher motives, he had been unconsciously fostering the seeds of skill and courage; and eventually his chief ambition was to distinguish himself by valour and ability in the field. He contributed largely from his own private resources the expenses of the war, and was elected my colleague in command, in which position he shewed me a still greater degree of attention and deference. When at length, victory declared itself on our side, through the visible intervention of the deity, we returned to Byzantium, and it was decreed, that the public thanks of the State should be conveyed to Hercules and Diana, for which purpose he was to proceed to Tyre, while I was despatched to this city. Before setting out Callisthenes took me by the hand and related every particular respecting Calligone. 'Father,' he said, 'the impetuosity of youth led me away in the first instance; but in the course which since then, I have pursued, deliberate choice and principle have influenced my actions. I have scrupulously respected the maiden's honour, during a time of war and confusion when men are generally least inclined to deny themselves the indulgence of their desires. My intention is now to conduct her to her father's house, at Tyre; and then to claim her for my bride, at her father's hand, in accordance with the law. I have made an ample settlement upon her, and shall consider myself most fortunate, if he grants my suit; if, on the contrary, I meet with a repulse he will receive back his daughter as pure as when she left his home.'

"I will now read you a friendly letter, which—feeling anxious that the marriage should be concluded—I addressed to my brother, before the termination of the war, in which I mentioned the rank of Callisthenes, and bore testimony to his good birth, the honourable position which he had attained, and his eminent services in the field. If we gain our cause in the new trial moved by Thersander, I propose, first of all to sail to Byzantium, and afterwards to proceed to Tyre."

Clinias came to us next day, with the intelligence that Thersander had secretly left the city, that his object in appealing from the recent decision was but a pretext to gain time, and that he had no intention of following up the case. After waiting three days, the period appointed for taking fresh proceedings, we appeared before the President, and having satisfactorily proved by reference to the statutes, that Thersander had no longer any legal ground against us, we embarked and enjoyed a favourable voyage to Byzantium, where our long-desired nuptials took place. A short time after, we sailed to Tyre, which we reached two days after the arrival of Callisthenes, and where I found my father preparing to celebrate my sister's wedding on the following day. We were present on the occasion, and assisted at the religious ceremonial, offering up our united prayers that both our marriages might be crowned with happiness; and we arranged, after wintering at Ephesus, to proceed to Byzantium in the spring.

THE END

Discover more of your favorite classics with Bookfinity™.

- Track your reading with custom book lists.
- Get great book recommendations for your personalized Reader Type.
- Add reviews for your favorite books.
- AND MUCH MORE!

Visit **bookfinity.com** and take the fun Reader Type quiz to get started.

Enjoy our classic and modern companion pairings!